This book is a work of fiction. The names, characters, places, and incidents are products of the writer's imagination or have been used fictitiously and are not to be construed as real. Any resemblance to persons, living or dead, actual events, locale or organizations is entirely coincidental.

More in this series:

Ross Wynton, leader of WEST Protection. He's got a head for the tactical and an instinct for danger. Then in walks the one person who reminds him that he's also a man.

After a big breakthrough with her gene editing project, Doctor Pippa Hamlin is neck-deep in danger and threats. On the run, she turns to the only person she knows who can protect her—the hot cowboy crush from her gawky teen years. While she still burns for the man, she hopes he'll help her reach Seattle for a big conference without meeting more danger.

Discovering who is threatening Pippa becomes Ross's number one priority. So does easing that fear he sees in her beautiful hazel eyes...and fighting to keep his hands off her tallies is a close second.

Ross fears he's too distracted and missing something, while Pippa battles to keep her wits to fight for the medical discovery she believes in. Traveling with a sexy, alpha, muscled bodyguard who brings all the heat to places a nerdy doctor ignores is hard enough without wondering if Ross will save her—or break her.

RESCUED BY THE COWBOY

BY

Em Petrova

Chapter One

Ross raised the glass of whiskey to his lips, but he never got to take a sip because a sexy woman wearing only a red, sheer thong shoved his drink aside.

She grabbed him by the western string tie he wore and leaned in close. "You want a piece of this, sugar?" She lifted one dainty foot sporting a red stiletto with feathers and planted it on the chair between his thighs, an inch from his balls.

His brothers, a couple cousins and his lifelong buddies at the table hooted and started tossing dollar bills his direction. Music pulsed and the women dancing onstage looked like disco balls with colored lights hitting their scanty costumes. Two were completely naked.

"Who picked this place for our weekly meeting anyway?" He snagged a handful of crumpled bills off the table. The dancer swished around to present her ass. With a coy glance over her shoulder, she bent over for him.

"Stick the bills in her thong!" his brother called when Ross sat immobile for a heartbeat too long.

He pulled the string out of the crack of her ass and wedged the bills under it. When he let it snap back in place, she whipped to face him with a glare.

She sashayed to the next table and straddled a businessman who was three sheets to the wind and probably had more money to waste.

Ross took his whiskey in hand and relished the slow burn slipping into his stomach. Christ, what a week. The guys who made up WEST Protection probably thought that holding their weekly meeting at a strip club would be a good way to unwind. But he didn't need a silk-covered ass waving her goods in his face to let loose.

Hell, he partied at least once a...

He thought long and hard about the last time he knocked down more than a drink or two or took a beautiful woman up against a wall. His brows scrunched, and he caught his little brother, Boone, looking at him.

"What are you starin' at?" He slugged down his whiskey and breathed through the flames.

"You didn't even look twice at that woman. She was waving her ass in your face! Did you even notice her clit was pierced?" Boone's white Stetson flashed with rainbow lights from the nearby stage.

"She had her clit pierced? How did I miss that?" His other little brother jumped to his feet and waved at the dancer to come back, but she simply blew him a kiss and moved on to another table.

"Shiiiiieeet, Ross. Running a company's making you old before your time." Boone motioned to a waitress to bring the table another round of Jameson. They'd shoved together four tables to make enough room for all ten of them working for WEST Protection security company.

Wynton, Shanie and Trace made up three of the letters of WEST. A short year ago, Ross, his cousin and his best buddy had formed the company that served the Western part of the US, and Ross's brothers jumped on board.

But only he seemed to be on task tonight. The guys were all either drinking, eyeing up beautiful women or both.

Maybe Boone was right—he *was* getting old before his time. But that happened to men who were driven to reach goals, right? His plan to scale up in the course of a year had exploded them onto the map, and now they couldn't even handle the calls they were receiving for security details, requests for personal protection officers and even help with guarding identities over the internet with their tech branch.

Wait until he told the guys about putting his next plan into action in order to take over the western US before spreading south.

Boone said something to him, and he blinked away his thoughts. "What was that?"

"You got too much manure in your ears, brother! If you're not on the ranch, you've got your head in a business plan or a case file. I said that dancer was waving at you from across the room."

He didn't bother to look. He wasn't interested in a woman who would wiggle her ass in the face of any man waving a buck. He sipped his whiskey and kicked back instead, watching his employees' interest in the scheduled meeting fade fast.

A dancer with big, perky tits headed their way, and all nine of his men whipped off their white Stetsons in her honor. Ross grunted, watching their antics as they plied her with money in trade for a peek at those big, hard nipples up close.

They needed to discuss so many things. The agenda he'd memorized floated away as he realized they weren't going to talk about protecting the governor from death threats, or even how to reduce the hundreds he received a day to a dozen. There wasn't an opportunity to go over details about security at the banks being hit with armed robberies or the countless security systems they were being paid to plug holes in.

The dancer moved on, and the guys placed their hats on their heads.

He tugged the brim of his own white Stetson, a trademark of WEST Protection, and raised his voice. "I have an announcement."

They all stopped talking and focused on him.

"I received a call from a woman who heads the planning team for the Grammys."

4

Nobody spoke.

"As in Grammy Wynton?"

Ross's lips twisted. "Not that type o' Grammy. I mean *the* Grammys. The big awards that happen annually."

Everyone blinked at him. All except for Boone, who stared at Ross as though he'd lost the ability to close his eyelids.

"You got...us a job...working security...for...the...Grammys?" Boone spaced out the words in a slow drawl.

He shook his head. "Nothing's finalized. No contracts signed."

"But they'll offer," Boone put in with stone-cold conviction.

Ross ducked his head in the Wynton nod handed down through the men of his family, along with a deep dimple in each of their cheeks. "Looks like it might happen. And if it does, we need more men. The best of the best, ya hear?" He pointed to his youngest brother Noah.

"Damn, brother, I admit I never believed you when you said WEST would be the biggest security company in the US." His middle brother Josiah pinned a stare on him.

"Not yet we aren't. And if we do reach the top—"

"Which we will," interjected Boone.

Ross went on, "Then we can't get lazy. We have to actually *be* the best. We haven't invested in all this

5

training, infrastructure, top-of-the-line computer systems and other high-priced gear only to let it all go with laziness."

"Look around you, Ross. Is there a single man here you'd call lazy?" Josiah spoke up.

If their determined expressions and muscled shoulders didn't say enough, he'd witnessed firsthand how damn lethal every man seated at this table was. Upon inception of the company, the first thing he did was fly everyone to Michigan to a top facility for training with elite soldiers from all over the world. At this point, they could handle everything including hostage rescues, reconnaissance, military combative techniques and could even treat trauma patients. And that was only the bodyguard division. The tech team had their own top training.

He started to answer Josiah, but his phone vibrated on the table next to his hand. He glanced at the number and didn't recognize it.

But he never let a call go. As a result, he listened to a lot of spam calls about his car's extended warranty. Often, the people who contacted him were clients sent to him by word of mouth.

"That the girl you were twirling around the dancefloor the other night, Ross?" his brother teased.

"Don't you guys know I'm older than my years and my personal life's in the shitter?" His comment had them all laughing. He snatched the phone on the second buzz and brought it to his ear.

"Ross Wynton."

"Uh...Ross?" The feminine voice came off as breathy, but maybe it was the music drowning her out.

"Yes, who is this?"

"It's Pippa."

He froze. He only knew one woman named Pippa.

"Pippa Hamlin."

His brain threw up a mental file of her containing her image and description. Pippa, daughter of his father's best friend. Last he'd heard, she graduated Yale or some other Ivy League school with magna cum laude and a degree in molecular something or other. He hadn't seen her since a big family barbecue when her family came from Seattle to visit his in Stone Pass, Montana. He couldn't recall much about that last gathering besides her being in that colt-like stage of her teens where guys didn't take notice.

That and she'd taken a fall off a horse, despite convincing him and his brothers that she could ride.

"Pippa?" He stood and wove his way through the club to the exit so he could hear her better. Passing several dancers who stopped to wink at him, he listened to the silence projecting into his ear on the other end of the line.

Once he burst outside into the cold, pine-scented Montana air, he said, "Can you hear me?"

"Yes."

7

Her voice still came out too soft.

"Is everything all right?"

A beat of silence followed. Then she said, "No. All wrong. I'm boarding flight 68 to Montana right now. I need you to pick me up at the airport."

His protective senses kicked in. "Pippa, where are you? What's going on?"

Another long pause and then her whisper sent shivers through him. "I'm being followed, Ross."

* * * * *

Pippa gripped the armrests as the jet angled toward the runway. She hated landings. And taking off. She hated planes, and now she had a brand-new terror of airports.

Fleeing Detroit was the only option, though. At first, things came up missing in her office — her favorite pair of earrings that her momma gave her after she graduated from Yale. She shouldn't have left them on her desk, but nobody went in the small, cramped space off the lab where she worked.

Next, a photo on her corkboard vanished. Since it was a photo of her with an old girlfriend on a camping trip, she started looking to the men in the lab. Maybe one was interested in her or the friend? Or perhaps the tack fell out and the cleaning personnel swept up the photo.

But then came the notes. Two in total, which wasn't many, except they shot her through with black

8

fear, and she was pretty sure the company frowned upon death threats.

When she spotted the slip of paper on top of her data printouts, she'd nearly passed out.

I got rid of others like you.

Breathing hard, she crumpled the paper in her fist, and heart pounding, looked at her surroundings, but nobody had been around her at the time.

Then the second threat hit this afternoon. This one couldn't be mistaken for somebody wanting to foist her from her job overseeing a special gene project. *I will kill you* was pretty self-explanatory.

With her bowels watery and her heart racing, she'd quickly gathered her belongings from her office and left for the day. She even managed not to run out the doors and across the parking lot to her car, though in retrospect, she didn't know how when she was so shaken.

The only thought burning through her brain was to find a person to help her. The police would ask a lot of questions she didn't have answers to. They'd stir things up at the lab by interrogating her coworkers. In the end, one name popped into her mind.

Ross Wynton.

His name had been brought up at Thanksgiving dinner at her parents' house in Seattle. He'd started some security company specializing in personal protection, and it'd taken off immediately.

She didn't stop to think when she ran to her apartment to throw some clothes in a bag and purchase a flight before hastening to the airport. She hadn't considered calling Ross *first*. But holding a calm phone call with the man to share her fears wasn't possible—not when someone in her city, her *lab* wanted her dead.

After she was on her way and felt she could breathe a little easier, she was attacked.

When she heard something heavy like a trash can being shoved across the airport restroom floor, she didn't question why. Her logical brain told her it was a janitor taking out the trash. But the minute she opened the stall door and faced a man, all logical thought flew out her ear, and her reflexes kicked in.

He yanked her out of the stall and locked an arm around her neck. She still felt her heels dragging across the tile floor. With her air cut off and stars blasting in front of her eyes like a fireworks display, her training kicked in. She hadn't spent two years studying with top scientists in her field in Japan without learning a martial art.

Aikido came to her rescue, and with all her strength, she'd used her body as a lever to lift the man and flip him. When he slammed off the floor and lay still, she feared she might have killed him.

No such luck.

In a blink, he came at her a second time, this time with a handgun with a long barrel, and she'd seen enough action flicks to know it was a silencer.

She could turn and flee, but he'd only come after her. So she steeled herself for round two, and when he lay on the floor again, this time with his eyes rolled up in his head, she didn't hesitate to run.

The long strap of her computer bag stuck out from under the stall door. She grabbed it and fled, leaving behind her carryon. Since she'd already gone through security, she was clear to board, and she jumped on that plane faster than she ever thought possible.

Which was how she ended up in Bozeman Airport with bumps, bruises and only her precious laptop with her personal research concerning the new gene project and a miasma of fear clouding her.

The jet taxied and came to a stop. Long minutes later she followed the rest of the passengers down the aisle, throwing covert glances around her for more attackers. She gripped her bag tight and pushed down the burning bile from everything that happened.

In the airport, she paused to throw a look around. She didn't expect Ross to be standing there holding a WELCOME PIPPA sign, but seeing his face would be nice.

Releasing a shaky sigh, she followed the herd of people to the baggage claim. There was safety in numbers, right? Nobody would jump out and attack her with a chance of being caught.

Though she didn't have any luggage, Ross could be waiting there for her, just as his family had waited for hers in the days when they visited.

The last time, she'd been fifteen. Seeing the huge, hunky Wynton boys hadn't eased her gawkiness or shyness one bit, and she hadn't set eyes on any of them since. She finished high school a year and a half early and went straight into college. While her family continued to see the Wyntons for fly-fishing trips, she hadn't made it.

So she'd taken a huge chance on Ross being the good man his father was and coming to her rescue.

Being above average height for a woman, she didn't have to crane her neck to see over the group. When she spotted a white cowboy hat, her lungs gave out and she couldn't find any air to draw back in. Two people in front of her moved, giving her a clear view of Ross Wynton.

He was even taller than her—and taller than last time she'd seen him. Broader too, but she recognized that twinkle in his dark green eyes as the same one she'd seen when he teased her after falling off a horse and into a thorn bush that last summer they were together.

In a few long-legged strides, he reached her. She looked up at his face and neither of them moved. Did they embrace? Their mothers and fathers did. But that felt too far from her comfort zone, so she stuck out her hand.

Ross enveloped it in his callused grip. "Pippa, we're going to get your luggage and then you're going to stick by my side and do everything I tell you to as we walk to my truck."

A small shudder ran down her spine. "Okay, but...I don't have any luggage."

He glanced down at the computer bag slung across her body and focused on her fingers fastened around the case.

She tried to loosen her grasp and a bit of blood rushed into her fingers after holding on so tight.

Without another word to ask why she'd traveled all the way from Detroit with only the clothes on her back, he took her by the elbow and steered her through the crowd gathering at the baggage claim.

The warmth of his fingers sank through the layers of her top — she'd also left her jacket in the restroom — and offered enough comfort that she was able to draw a full breath into her lungs. They burned at being starved for air. All her medical training taught her shallow breathing came with a big hit of adrenaline, but in the moment, what did that matter?

Now that she could let down her guard a little and put her safety in the hands of Ross Wynton, her adrenaline level dropped too.

She started to shiver, and by the time they hit the exit, her teeth chattered.

He shot her a look, two hard brackets appearing on either side of his tense lips. Wordlessly, he removed his coat, a thick canvas. When he settled it around her shoulders, she inhaled the scent of him and her stomach fluttered at his body heat trapped in the fibers.

As he steered her through the parking lot to a truck bearing the Wynton Ranch logo of a W inside a circle, her legs started to give out.

"Lean on me." The rough grumble would have filled her adolescent heart with excitement at fifteen, but now it punched her with the realization that she was really here in Montana, running for her life.

He unlocked the door and motioned her in. She managed to settle in the leather seat, aware that he locked her in with a flick of the key fob as he circled to the driver's door. Why? In case somebody got to her while he walked around?

Her insides heaved, and she folded her hands on her laptop case to still them from shaking. Ross again unlocked the doors to glide into the seat with all the grace of the cowboy sliding into a saddle.

The door locks clicked once more and he started the engine. Her insides jittered. What if he thought her insane? She couldn't blame him really. The number of times she questioned her sanity while in flight tallied in the double digits.

As he whipped out of the lot headed toward the parking pay station, he remained silent. At the gate, he held up an ID and the security officer waved them through without paying.

Pippa took all this in with her scientist's mind. Observation was a major step in the process of an experiment, so she took note of the truck interior, the early morning Montana landscape of snow-covered mountains and heavy clouds banked on the horizon. She pulled in the scent of leather, an underlying hint of the ranch she remembered...and the spice of the man at the wheel.

That brought her to observing Ross. From the corner of her eye, she studied his same strong features and the white Stetson their family favored wearing like some kind of ranch family dress code. But his features appeared stronger. His jaw an angled slice of mountain rock brushed with a five o'clock shadow.

If he'd filled out in those areas, his body had doubled her expectations. His muscled chest stretched the black cotton T-shirt, and his biceps fought against the stitches around the sleeves. One had actually popped, and a short thread kept drawing her eye.

"All right. Talk to me, Pippa." He cast her a look she couldn't read.

Staring at her white knuckles against the black leather of her bag, she sucked in a stabilizing breath.

Without waiting for her to start speaking, he fired a question at her. "Why don't you have any luggage?"

"I left it in the bathroom in Detroit. I lost my purse and jacket as well."

He whipped his head to pierce her in his intense gaze. "Okay, start at the top, with when you decided to call me. What happened?"

She saw why his security company was climbing the ranks as one of the top in the US. He owned a situation—always did. When she fell off the horse into the thorn bush, he'd raced back to help her up, scolded his younger brother Josiah for laughing at her, and proceeded to pick thorns out of her arms.

"I'm not sure if you know but my work involves gene editing."

"My father mentioned it."

She nodded. "I work in a lab. Most of the time I'm alone, but I have some assistants working with me on various projects."

"I'm listening."

"So it was odd when things started coming up missing in my office."

"Such as?" He ramped up the speed on the open highway that would lead to the Wynton Ranch.

"My favorite earrings my mother gave me. And a photo of me and my best friend."

"Could you have misplaced them? Or they fell off your desk and got swept up by cleaning people?"

He didn't believe her. Hell, she hardly believed her own suspicions.

Shaking her head, she continued, "I received death threats."

He whipped his head around, his expression masked. "What kind of threats?"

"They're notes."

"Do you have them?"

"One, yes." She started to reach into the zippered pocket of her bag.

"Don't get it out. I don't want you to touch it any more than you already have."

"You believe there may be fingerprints on it?"

"I'll have my guys run a check."

"You can do that?"

He sliced a glance at her that reminded her this wasn't the boy she once knew. Ross was a man of power and skill, and every word he spoke reflected that change.

Folding her fingers around the bag, she stared at the landscape and tried to pick up the pieces of her life. Her neck hurt from her attacker's stronghold, and it was difficult to swallow.

"Do you have some water?" she rasped.

He removed one big hand from the steering wheel, leaned toward her and reached behind her seat. He withdrew a bottle, cold from the low temps.

She took it and sipped slowly, trying not to choke around the lump lodged in her throat that she knew from many classes in anatomy and health to be swelling.

"Better?" he asked after a minute.

She nodded. "I knew you'd carry water. I remember your family was always prepared for any circumstance."

"Gotta be in this country. Now. Tell me how you got that bruise on your wrist."

Startled, she looked down at the purple smudge blossoming across her wrist bone. Her stomach pitched at the memory of the fight in the restroom.

"I was attacked."

"Jesus Christ. Where?"

"In the airport. It's how I lost my belongings. I don't even have my wallet or ID."

"What the hell happened?"

Her stupid response to the question was to flush. "I had to...pee."

He made a strangled noise in his throat, and she wondered if he really did still have more of that boy she'd known buried inside him than she first guessed. The one who chose horses over swoony, moony-eyed girls who believed him the boyfriend material of the century.

"Go on," he muttered.

"When I opened the stall door, a man was standing there. He grabbed me around the neck." She lifted a hand to trail her fingertips over her throat.

"How the hell did you get free?"

"Aikido."

"Come again?"

"The Japanese martial art."

"I know what it is. But you know it?"

"I spent some years in Asia studying it. It...came in handy today." Her throat clogged off more at the knowledge of what might have befallen her if she hadn't been able to defend herself. "I took the man down and ran for it. I jumped on the plane and came straight to you."

He glanced in the rearview mirror for the third time in a mile, which set her on edge. A peek at the side mirror showed her they were alone on this stretch of road. He was just being cautious. Doing his job. Using skills she put her faith in.

"Ross, what do I do?"

He let go of the wheel again and rested his hand on the back of hers. Some desperate need to feel the touch of a friend struck, and she twisted her hand up to grip his. He didn't let her go, and she clung to the warmth and strength emanating from him.

"We'll figure it out. You're safe now, Pippa."

Hearing her name fall from his lips in that rough rumble—rougher in manhood—flipped something inside her. Maybe neither of them had changed. She still held a flicker of a flame for the cowboy.

Now more than a cowboy. He was an entrepreneur, and judging by those layers of muscle stacked on his body, he'd trained to fight.

"Tell me how you got the idea to start your company," she said.

He looked at her with a crease between his long brows. "Another time, Pippa. Let's get you to the ranch first."

He said *to the ranch*. What she heard was: *to the safety of the ranch.*

She glanced in the mirror again. Nobody followed, but she had some distance to go to shake the person who wanted her dead.

Chapter Two

Pippa was not the little girl he remembered.

When he last saw her, her teeth had been too big for her face, and his brother might have mentioned her resembling one of the horses at one point. His other brothers and cousins had laughed, but Ross put them in their place with a few threats to make them as toothless as babies if they didn't shut up.

She also used to be tall, with arms and legs she didn't seem quite able to control. Now she was even taller—she must be five feet ten—and she'd filled out in all the right areas. Her brown hair was still pulled into a ponytail, just like when they were kids, but it appeared thicker, shinier.

She still wore glasses too, though her hazel eyes no longer appeared owlish from behind the lenses. Instead, the dark frames lent her a studious—and maybe mysterious—air.

One thing he recalled from her visits to Montana was her shyness, and while some of that seemed to have trickled away, he still felt her hesitation when it came to talking to him. He had to pull each word out of the woman.

As he drove, he considered her story. She was never prone to fanciful tales in the past, and that bruise she wore, along with her skittish nature, proved something had happened to her. But death threats against a woman who worked in a lab seemed a little off to him.

His first protocol was to get her to a safe place, and nowhere safer than the Wynton Ranch existed. Between him and his brothers, not to mention his very protective parents and a dozen or so bad-ass ranch hands who'd kick the shit out of trespasser and ask questions later, Pippa was in good hands.

Casting a look at her tense pose, he struggled to find some words to ease her fears. He might be trained to soothe flighty clients—horses too—but knowing this woman changed some dynamic for him.

Almost as if he could easily cross a boundary. Hell, she might as well be a little cousin to him, they'd grown up so close. He'd looked forward to the Hamlins' visits each fall when the trout started biting.

As he glanced at her again, he took note of her simple white button-down blouse and the hint of pale, freckled flesh above the buttons. Her breasts swelled into way more than the tiny bumps she once sported.

He twisted his gaze away. Okay, so maybe not like a little cousin. A family friend. He'd leave it at that.

22

She issued a small gasp, and he followed her gaze to the gates of the Wynton Ranch. "You changed the gates!" Her throat had a soft, husky quality heard in woman who smoked and drank. He couldn't picture her doing either of those things, so the changes must be natural.

He directed his attention to the gates. "Yeah, we installed these a few years ago. Lots of trouble with tourists coming up here and thinking they can just drive down any old road." He eased the truck up to the closed black iron gates. Two halves created their ranch brand in the center.

As soon as the camera identified his truck as being one of theirs, the locks clicked and the gates slowly swung open, parting the W in the center into a V in a half circle on either side.

Pippa watched the gates as they passed through and twisted in her seat to look out the back at them shutting.

"Things have changed around here."

His lips twitched. "We finally stepped into the next century. A hundred years of Wyntons working this ranch showed us to work smarter, not harder."

"I hope not all has changed. I'd hate to see robot cows walking around or something."

Her statement brought a smile to his face. "We haven't gone that far. Everything around here is still flesh and blood. But we did step up security."

23

As he navigated the long road leading to the spread, he tried to see it through Pippa's eyes. She hadn't been here in what? Fifteen years? That'd put her around thirty. Too old for fears of the boogieman, but could her small world of laboratories and experiments keep her sheltered for reality?

Fields lined either side of the road and stretched as far as the eye could see. Clear up to the mountains.

"Where's the cattle?" she asked and then cleared her throat.

He looked closer at her. Maybe that husky quality derived from something else. He needed to get her to the ranch and examine her more. "They're wintering over the ridge. Sunny side of the slopes this time o' year."

"I guess I've never visited the ranch this time of year."

"No." As they crested a small rise in the road, the full ranch popped into view. The big house was sided with stained wood and a stone face echoed the three chimneys, also clad in stone. Heavy timbers peaked over the front door, which was black like the gates and roofs of every building on the property.

"A lot of changes," she breathed.

"Updates."

"I always thought this place was beautiful, but now it looks like something out of a film set."

"My momma will be pleased to hear you say that."

She turned to him, blinking. "I didn't think about seeing your family!"

He chuckled. "You ask for me, you get the lot of us. They'll be mighty pleased to see ya too. But Pippa."

Her gaze met his, a shadow creeping into the greenish gold depths.

"Don't say anything about what happened to you. I'll do that."

She nodded and issued a slow breath. "How do I explain the fact I came with no luggage?"

"I'll get Corrine on the matter. My sister loves to shop her heart out, and this is right in her wheelhouse."

"Corrine. She was so little last time I saw her. How old is she now?"

"Just celebrated her twenty-first birthday last weekend."

"Twenty-one..." She shook her head, sending her ponytail swaying over her spine.

He saw her nerves kick in as they pulled up in front of the garage. She didn't move to exit the vehicle, and he faced her. "It's okay, Pip."

Her eyes widened at the nickname. "Nobody's called me that in years."

"I'll always think of you as Pip." He climbed out of the truck and by the time he reached the passenger door, she stood outside it. As he approached, he took in everything about her, from the black boots she wore, jeans that weren't worn from hard work but in a dyeing process, and her white top, slightly crinkled from her flight and ordeal.

His gaze zeroed in on her throat, though. A blue stripe banded across her neck, marring her freckled skin. His gut twisted, and a fury hit him he wasn't expecting.

"Fucking hell. Your throat," he ground out, stepping closer to her.

She lifted a hand. "Is it bad?"

"Bad? Hell, Pippa. You didn't tell me your attacker tried to strangle you!" He reached out and flicked her collar aside to see it in full detail. By full morning it'd be technicolor. No wonder her voice sounded that way.

She froze and dropped her gaze to his chest, refusing to meet his eyes.

He let his arm swing to his side. "Well, at least I don't have to carry your luggage inside. C'mon."

Her relieved expression told him that his joke had the effect he was going for. As he led her to the house, he kept her on his left so he could shoot with his right—his training so ingrained in him that he didn't even think about it until they reached the front door. He ushered her in.

When she paused in the entryway, he shook his head. "Don't take your boots off. You remember the rules of the house. No mud, you're fine."

"I might have some snow from walking across the driveway—" she began.

He planted his hand on her lower back and nudged her toward the living room.

* * * * *

Pippa's breath caught at her first sight of the space she'd spent a lot of time in as a child. Soaring ceilings with rustic, exposed support beams. Three huge chandeliers dripping in tiers of glass set at perfect intervals. Tall windows showered the room in sunlight, made brighter by reflecting off the snow outside.

Two leather sofas faced each other over a coffee table almost the size of a twin bed. At one end of the table sat a stack of magazines she knew from memory would be on the topics of fly fishing, cowboys and ranching. In the center sat a huge spray of dried flowers as artful as ones that sat in expensive hotels in Europe.

One thing about Mrs. Wynton, she had a lot of class.

The room invited a person to sit—another testimony to the Wyntons' famous hospitality. But Pippa stood with her boots rooted to the hand-scraped hardwood floors, her pulse thrumming with anxiety.

Ross threw her a look. "You good for a minute? I'll go find Momma."

She nodded and watched him stride from the room with all the confidence and bearing of a king. Which he might as well be. His family name was known as far as California, for the prime angus beef they sold to elite restaurants there.

A high-pitched cry sounded from somewhere in the house, and seconds later a woman ran into the living room. Pippa met Mrs. Wynton's bright eyes but jumped when the woman let out another scream.

"You *are* here! Oh my God! Pippa, my dear woman. My land, you're so beautiful!"

Heat climbed into her cheeks at the woman's outburst, and then Mrs. Wynton ran up and threw her arms around her.

Enveloped by the scent of all the things she associated with this place, Pippa closed her eyes and embraced her in return. Tears threatened, but she swallowed them down. This was the closest thing she had to hugging her own momma, and the warm welcome filled her with affection.

Mrs. Wynton pulled away to look at her. She was tall as well, but not as tall as Pippa. A quick study of her face revealed more lines of age but the same health and vitality from leading a life of exercise, fresh air and the family she loved.

"I'm so shocked to see you. I thought Ross was fooling me." She threw a look around for her son who did like to prank her in his youth, as Pippa remembered.

"It's so good to see you, Mrs. Wynton."

"Oh dear, we're past those sorts of formalities. Your parents enforced the rule that you call me Mrs. Wynton. Call me Ginny. Please."

"Ginny." Her heart bloomed with warmth, but it didn't thaw the coil of fear she'd traveled here with.

"Pippa could use something to eat and drink, Momma." He eyed Pippa. His eyes conveyed a question. *You'll be okay?*

She nodded to both the sustenance and the question.

Touched even more that he did care for her well-being, she followed Mrs. Wynton—it'd be hard to think of her as Ginny after all these years—into the spacious kitchen.

"Momma, is Corrine around?"

"In the barn with her horse. Where else?" She beamed a smile on Pippa and waved for her to sit down.

Pippa's knees felt wobbly as she moved to the heavy wood barstool and sat. Ross left the room. She watched him vanish through the doorway. Right before he walked away, he'd glanced at her throat—a pointed reminder to keep quiet about her ordeal?

Wanting to conceal her bruises from Ginny, she waited until her back was turned and buttoned her shirt up to her throat. She hoped that would hide the worst of the bruise.

"Coffee or something cold?" Ginny asked.

"Something cold please." It would feel good on her throat.

Ginny puttered to the big stainless steel refrigerator that could hold half a beef and unearthed a pitcher of iced tea. Pippa's mouth watered. She remembered the famous sweet tea on the Wynton Ranch, made with just the right amount of sugar and a hint of mint.

"I can fix you eggs and bacon if you're up for it."

"I'm not that hungry, but thank you."

When Ginny set a glass in front of her, along with a plate of fresh-baked cookies, Pippa choked back her tears.

She hadn't cried once since she received that death threat. Not after she fled from the lab or following her attack. Now she teared up at a plate of cookies.

Through a blur, she reached for one. "Thank you, Mrs. — Ginny."

The woman eyed her. "I see you have something pressing on you, honey, and I'm dying to help. But my son warned me not to ask any questions."

Bringing a cookie to her lips, she nodded. Feeling like a child with her tears consoled by cookies, she nibbled the edge, but her appetite had been left in that lab when she found the words *I will kill you* scrawled on a note.

She set the cookie on the napkin and lifted her tea instead. "Tell me about the family. I feel so out of touch."

Ginny settled in for one of those chats she and Pippa's mother used to have. Actually, they still did — she knew her family made the trip to Montana every year at the fly hatch for a spot of fishing.

"Well, you saw Ross. Bossy as ever." Shooting Pippa a wink, she raised her voice for her son to overhear in the event he was nearby. "As you might know, he started a security company with his friend Silas Shanie and his cousin Mathias Trace. Then he brought his other cousin Landon and his brothers on board, so all four of my boys are out doing dangerous jobs more often than I like to hear about. Good thing they don't supply me with details." She stopped to sip her tea — being a mother of this crew was thirsty work. "Corrine is helping on the ranch, but more and more Ross is giving her small jobs with WEST Protection."

Like sending the young woman to purchase a wardrobe for Pippa.

"Oh! You might have heard my youngest son Noah found a wonderful young woman to settle down with. Maya Ray is from right here in Stone Pass. They rent a house on the outskirts of town."

"That's wonderful. How funny that your youngest is the first to settle." Her mind wandered to Ross. With his rugged good looks, he must have women flocking to him. He was smart too.

31

She pushed her glasses up her nose and offered a small smile, the most she could muster.

"We love having Maya Ray around, and when you meet her, I'm sure you'll get along very well."

"I'm sure..." Her voice sounded as a rasp. Automatically, she lifted a hand and toyed with her collar.

Ginny followed her movement, and a crease — similar to Ross's — deepened between her eyes. Pippa braced herself for some questions to follow, but her friend thankfully remained silent.

After her refreshments, Ginny showed her to the bathroom, where she splashed water on her face and tried to put her hair in order. As she removed the elastic band from her ponytail, her gaze lit on her reflection. Blue streaks crossed her neck. She knew much of the bruising she'd caused herself, when she used that maneuver to flip her attacker. His body weight had hung off her neck — little wonder she was bruised.

Running her fingers through her hair to pull out the worst of the tangles from her long, exhausting day, she studied her face in the mirror. Her eyes were too wide, conveying her shock. She ducked her head and splashed more water on them.

The Wyntons must think her crazy to show up here after fifteen years. Yet they'd opened their arms to her.

She only hoped she could explain before Ginny called Pippa's mother. The last thing she wanted was her family worrying over her safety. Being here was more than nice—it was exactly what she needed. Since she didn't have to worry about someone jumping out and trying to kill her, she could focus on devising a plan.

After she placed her glasses on, she went to find Ginny. Or Ross.

She found both, seated in the kitchen, speaking quietly. Their gazes landed on her as she entered, but she was looking at Ross when she entered. His eyes traveled over her hair and face, down to the buttoned-up shirt covering her bruising.

"I'll send Corrine in to find you when she arrives," Ginny said to him. Then she started out of the kitchen. As she passed Pippa, she squeezed her arm and continued on without saying a word.

Pippa met Ross's gaze. He twitched his head toward the big table and chairs. After they were seated across from each other, her nerves kicked in. His silence and authority didn't help matters, and she suddenly felt fifteen again.

"Corrine's gone into town to find you some clothes and toiletries."

"I appreciate you sending her. I'll pay you back."

He cast off her offer with a wave. "We need to talk frankly. I need to know everything, Pippa. Every single detail you can recall, even if it seems unimportant."

She gave a slow nod. She started at the top, when she found her mother's earrings missing.

"Why weren't you wearing the earrings?"

"Sometimes I take them off before an experiment. There's so much protective gear to wear in order to keep me safe and the experiments uncontaminated."

He accepted her response and she continued, moving to the missing photograph. "Give me the name of your friend in the photograph."

She did, and he typed it into his phone. She watched his face closely, but he didn't give away anything about what he was looking at.

Setting aside his phone, he met her stare. "Tell me about the first threat."

Scraping her hair off her face, she whispered the words written on the slip of paper. "I got rid of others like you." Her stomach twisted, and she focused on the wood grain of the table as a way to center herself from the dizziness overtaking her.

Ross didn't speak, his face an unreadable mask. Several seconds passed before he spoke again.

He plied her with questions about what happened after she received the note. Did she keep it? Did anyone approach her afterward, or did life go on as normal?

She responded to everything as thoroughly as possible.

34

"Tell me about where you live."

"An apartment complex."

"Security?"

"A doorman."

He nodded. "Do you know his name?"

She blinked. "Yes, Eric has the day shift and Michael the night. Why would you need that?"

"Because I'm going to talk to them."

A shiver snaked down her spine at Ross's tone — soft, a little gritty. Deadly.

"You can't suspect either man of this."

"Everyone is a suspect until I say they're not. But I have other reasons for wanting to talk to them. I want to know about the building's security, and whether or not anybody's asked about you."

Her stomach pitched. She set her elbows on the table and dropped her head into her hands. "This has gone so far."

"We'll figure it out, Pippa. I've never failed yet."

She jerked her gaze to his. "I never doubted, Ross. It's why I called you."

His stare slipped over her face. A strange twist of awareness in her stomach replaced the sick dread.

"Now." He paused. "Tell me about your work. Is it sensitive at all?"

"I... Yes, it's sensitive."

He waited to hear more, but she didn't know how to say she'd made such an enormous breakthrough in the world of gene studies that it would help not only a few people but save the lives for a massive number of the population.

"Still shy." Ross's statement made her jerk. He sat back in his chair to regard her. "Dare I say humble too? I don't think all scientists possess that trait—they want credit for their discoveries, and here you sit completely silent when I ask about your work."

"I don't want fame. I only want to help people."

He tapped a finger on the table. "Tell me about that."

"About four months ago I had a big breakthrough. I told you I'm involved with gene editing…and I'll spare you all the terminology, but I'll say what I discovered will change the face of medicine."

He tapped a blunt fingertip on the table again. "Like cancer?"

"Cancer treatments, immunological medicines, the treatments of birth defects and even extending human lifespan."

He gave her a direct look. "So it's big."

She blew out a ragged breath. She still couldn't believe it herself. This was one of the top finds of the century. "Yes."

"Do you work with others on this project?"

"I had two assistants. They ran data for me and compiled information."

"Give me their names."

She did, and again he placed them in his phone.

"Did you ever feel threatened by either of your assistants, even if it was just a bad feeling?" he asked.

She racked her brain for such an experience, but nothing came to mind. "No. No, I never felt anything but a normal camaraderie with my assistants."

"Who owns the lab? Give me names."

This went on and on, until her brain felt like mush. She turned her head to stare at the landscape beyond the double doors. They led to a patio where their families shared so much food and fun. Now everything was coated in a layer of snow, but the beauty of the scenery soothed her soul.

When she turned her head, she found Ross staring at her. She swallowed hard. God, he was a rugged and beautiful man. All cowboy and strength and determination with enough muscle to cause her stomach to flutter. Add in the dark shadow sprouting on his squared jaw and the promise of a smile — and a glimpse of his Wynton dimple — and suddenly, she was a gawky teen crushing on an older boy who paid her no notice.

Uneasy with her thoughts, she pushed her glasses up.

"You've given me a lot of information to process, Pippa. I'll start digging into the backgrounds of each person you named, as well as your company and its employees. What you've discovered is something other people will want. Other companies, even other countries."

"Yes."

"You've provided a motive for the crime and made yourself a target."

She pulled up straight in her seat. "I was doing my job," she said with the heat his remark raised in her.

"Of course you were. But that doesn't mean you—" He received a text and cut off to read it. "Boone got called out, and he can't do the afternoon chores." He arched a brow at her. "Come with me? I'd like to keep talking to you. But if you're too tired…"

"I'm not. Besides, I haven't helped with ranch chores in a long time."

"You can wear one of Corrine's jackets. If you don't mind smellin' like a horse, that is."

For the first time since sitting down with him, a smile tickled at the corners of her mouth.

He outfitted her with a jacket and donned one of his own, the same thick canvas he'd given her outside the airport. For some reason, as she followed him to the barn, she couldn't stop thinking about slipping her arms around his shoulders and leaning against his strong body just to smell his male spice again.

"At least you've got on sensible boots."

She strode through the light snow beside him. "They always recommend shoes that can't fall off when you fly."

The tilt of his smile reflected in her heartrate. "And you adhere to all the rules, don't you, Pippa?"

Was he making fun of her? Sure, she was a rule follower—what was wrong with that?

"I wore these boots because they're the most comfortable I own. I never understood the FAA's reason for the recommendation. If you crash, losing a flip-flop's the least of your concerns."

His smile flashed again as they reached the barn. He handed her a shovel. "Remember how to muck out a stall?"

She chuckled, which sounded throatier than before, as if Ross took over her body whenever he was near. Such as a rise in her pulse and body temperature, and the lowering of her voice into something softer.

"Do I have to worry about one of your brothers shoving me into the manure pile?" she asked.

Another grin slanted her way. She curled her toes inside her boots and gripped the shovel handle tighter.

"If they were around, I'd have them do this job, not you. C'mon."

As he led her into the space, she was thrown back in time. Traditions and a love for family and friends mingled with the scents of straw and horses. She stopped in the center aisle between stalls to stare up at the beams of light streaming in through high windows. Aware of Ross stopping next to her, she flushed.

"I always loved this one horse. Maverick."

"Ole Mav? He's out in the pasture."

She blinked. "He's still alive?"

"Horses ain't like dogs. They live longer. I'll show you."

When they stepped out of the barn into the small pasture enclosed by new a black fence, she caught sight of the horse she'd fed carrots to and groomed on many occasions. His chestnut coat still gleamed in the sun as he gracefully bent to pluck hay from the bale.

"Oh, he's just as beautiful. He used to let me braid his mane."

"He sure is...and I remember." Ross watched Maverick and another horse keeping him company munching on the hay. A moment passed and he planted the point of his shovel into the snow. "Best get to work. Stalls won't clean themselves."

Chapter Three

Ross wheeled the barrow full of soiled straw into the allocated area and dumped it. This work was as familiar as breathing, and he could do it blindfolded. Which was why he loved the challenge he got with WEST Protection.

However, he could do without *this* challenge. When he started the company, he never thought he'd be protecting Pippa Hamlin.

At first, if he was honest, he didn't totally buy her story of being followed. Then one look at the bruises on her pale skin and he wanted to hunt down the people after her and snap their necks. One by one.

His reaction didn't make a lick of sense. Over the course of the year he'd been doing this job, he never felt such intense anger on behalf of his clients. Since the moment he spotted the fear creasing Pippa's eyes back in that airport, then the purple and blue bruises, he'd told himself that his response was due to her being like a kid sister to him.

But that got snatched by the late autumn wind each time he looked at her.

He stepped into the barn again. She worked in Maverick's stall, her pale brown, thick hair swishing on the shoulders of her borrowed coat.

"We need a plan."

She turned at his announcement.

"I have a feeling you're not talking about which stall to clean next." She moved to the door of the stall and faced him.

He nodded.

She drew in a breath. "I can start off the plan. I need to be in Seattle by Sunday."

His brows shot up. "To be with your family?"

"No. I'm speaking at a conference Monday morning. Genomics and Molecular Biology. I'd planned to stay with my parents for a long weekend and then head back to Detroit Tuesday morning. They expect me on Friday, but I think that's out the window."

He scuffed his boot on the floorboards. "This tosses another layer of meat onto the sandwich."

Her brows pinched. "Sandwich?"

"Yeah. My brothers laugh at me for comparing our jobs to sandwiches, but I really do see it that way. The bread's the danger, the meats and cheeses information that work together or against each other, and finally you sprinkle on lettuce, tomato, onion, pickles and so on to create one big case."

"And my going to Seattle is the meat?"

"That's right," he drawled.

She leaned on her shovel and brushed a wisp of hair off her face. "What kind of meat? Are we talking turkey or ham?"

His lips twitched. Nothing about her situation was in any way humorous, but the fact she could joke around made him remember her dry wit as a child. His brothers hadn't appreciated it, but since he was older, and more mature than his years even then, he did.

"Definitely ham." He liked what he saw far too much.

The previous night a sexy woman in a red thong with a pierced clit wiggled her ass in his face, and she didn't have a fraction of the effect on him that Pippa did at this minute—disheveled, tired, frightened...beautiful.

Shit. Rule one of personal protective services? Don't get involved with your ward.

Her link to his family already threw a heap of dirt over that rule. But this was more. Ross never lied to himself. He couldn't stand in front of Pippa and say he didn't feel attraction on a big level.

Bigger than any he'd felt in years, if he was a straight-talker—and he was.

This flashed through his mind in an instant, but it took him a minute to gather his words and the gumption to say them to her.

"Pippa..."

She waited.

"What do you say about one of my brothers taking over your case? I have a big contract to negotiate and a ton of things to manage with the company — " He broke off as he saw her expression.

He could only describe it as utter devastation.

Well, I did basically say she's less important than negotiating a contract. Goddammit.

Her lips wobbled and her eyes flooded with tears. Red patches hit her cheeks. But the look she gave him really did him in.

He stepped up to her. "Hell. I'm sorry, Pip. I shouldn't have suggested it. Forget I said anything. I'll figure it out, delegate more."

A step closer put them within touching distance. The urge to draw her into his arms twisted him up bad, but he resisted. Not only was she his ward, but she was his family friend. Crossing boundaries would be a disaster.

She stared at her boots for a long heartbeat, giving him a chance to study the faint freckles across her forehead, probably put there by the Montana sun. Finally, she glanced up and dashed a tear off her cheek. "I'm sorry. It's been a long day."

"It's me that's sorry." He started to reach to pull her into his arms.

"Ross! Oh here you are. Momma said to come and find you when I got home." Corrine's voice echoed down the long barn.

They both turned to his little sister, walking down the center aisle as if she strutted on a runway. Corrine may look like a rodeo queen, though she worked harder than most men on the ranch.

She didn't know it, but he couldn't be more glad to see her. This conversation with Pippa threw him into a world he had no clue how to navigate.

"Pippa, you remember Corrine."

She stepped out of the stall and hurried forward to embrace his sister. As she brushed past him, he caught her scent. What made him pull in a deep breath at that moment?

She smelled like…

Like apple blossoms.

And honey.

Something welled inside him, as if he'd known those scents all his life and she'd only just reminded him how much he loved them.

Shaking himself, he watched the women's reunion. Over Pippa's shoulder, his sister met his gaze. A question lingered in her eyes, but he only nodded.

She stepped back. "Is that my jacket?"

Pippa stammered, "Y-yes. Ross loaned it to me. I hope you don't mind."

"Of course not. And I'm jealous because you look better in it! But I did buy you a new one." His sassy fireball sister swung toward him. "Ross?"

"Why don't you go inside with Corrine? I'll finish up." And call a meeting with his team to fix a plan concerning his new ward.

Pippa faced him, and he gave her a nod and as much of a normal smile as possible when his insides felt like big, knotted ropes and a black cloud of disaster hung over him.

He definitely needed to talk this through.

As soon as Corrine led Pippa from the barn, he snatched his phone from his pocket and ordered everyone to the conference room.

"And I don't mean the damn strip club," he growled.

* * * * *

Deep in thought, Ross stared at the light dancing across the surface of the long walnut table. The WEST Protection headquarters was situated on the Wynton Ranch on a south-facing slope, so the room flooded with late morning sun.

The scrape of a chair on the floor brought his attention to Josiah. Behind him, the rest of his brothers, cousins and friends, all but Boone, filed into the conference room.

He waited until every man sat before he spoke. "I picked up an old friend at the airport. She requires protection."

Josiah's brows shot up. "Pippa?"

46

"How the hell did you hear that already? You weren't anywhere near the house when she arrived."

Josiah shot him a come-the-hell-on look. "Not as if it isn't my job to be observant and overhear things."

He removed his Stetson and set it on the table before him. "You talked to Corrine."

"Passed her on the way down the driveway — going to buy your new ward a wardrobe."

"I never should have trusted Corrine. She probably blabbed to everyone in Stone Pass that Pippa's here."

"Give her the benefit of the doubt, brother," Noah spoke up from the opposite end of the table. "The only people she'd say a word to is Josiah, Boone, or me."

Josiah bobbed his head.

"None of that matters right this minute. I called a meeting for another reason. I need one of you here to man the phones while I'm gone."

"Where are you going?" Josiah asked.

"Seattle."

"Flying?"

"Road trip." He couldn't see a way to fly with a woman who didn't have any identification, and getting clearances for a personal jet would take more time than he could waste. He went on, "We can't let this contract for the Grammys pass us by. It means putting our name at the top of the list of security services. Dammit, it's the worst possible time for me to leave."

"So hand her off to someone else," Josiah said.

"I can't do that." The panic reflected in her eyes when he suggested the same thing to her in the barn really touched him in a way he didn't want to think about.

"Which one of us is sitting around waiting for a phone call?" Josiah nodded toward Noah. "I say the youngest does it."

Noah rolled his eyes. "I thought the youngest always shovels the manure?"

"I just did that," Ross muttered, analyzing the field in his mind and the players on it. "Boone's on duty at the capital with the governor."

Josiah dipped his head in a nod.

"Silas, Landon, Mathias, you're working the bank."

"Yep," his lifelong friend Silas said.

"We were up all night installing firewalls. You woke me up to come here." Landon's homeless appearance reflected his sleepless night. He wore a ratty T-shirt with a few holes in it and sported a day's beard growth.

Ross grunted. "Pretty sure when I left the club, you guys were on your third whiskies."

"You're not wrong—but we went straight to work."

Ross tapped the table with his palm to indicate they were finished with the topic. "All this proves to me that we need to hire more people. Noah, keep on that while I'm gone. And Josiah, you get the honor of babysitting the phone."

His brothers exchanged glares.

"Can't we do rock, paper, scissors for it?" Josiah readied his hand.

Ross arched a brow.

"I had to try, Ross. You know I hate sitting around twiddlin' my thumbs."

He understood that sentiment, but he still needed Josiah here. Time was slipping by too quickly, and he wanted a strong plan in place.

"Josiah, I could use a route that isn't a straight shot to Seattle. No goat paths through the mountains either. The weather will be harsh enough this time of year."

"Got it."

"Also, I need you to find out everything you can about these names I'm sending you." He shot off the list he compiled from his discussion with Pippa and turned his attention to Landon. "How long will it take you to run some fingerprints for me?"

He straightened, looking suddenly more alert than five minutes before. "Just have to run them through the database for a match."

"Good. Follow me to the house and I'll give you the specimen." He stood, ready for action. The only other question in his mind was whether leaving first thing in the morning would be best. Pippa hadn't slept, and they had another long trip ahead. On the other hand, the sooner they got on the road the better.

He started out of the room, but thought of something and turned. "Josiah, I'll need you to back me up in Seattle."

"When do I arrive?"

"Sunday."

"You can count on me."

He met his brother's gaze. "I know I can."

As he left the headquarters and headed to the main house, his mind whirled with all the things he needed in place before their trip, supplies the least of their worries.

His top priority was finding out who was threatening Pippa's life.

* * * * *

Pippa watched Ross carry a case of water from a metal shelving unit in the garage to the back seat of the truck. He set it on the floor before returning to the shelf for more supplies. He grabbed two blankets and a mini cooler, adding those to the growing stash in the truck.

He tossed a couple heavy chains in the bed, and she arched a brow. "You already got tire chains."

"Couple extra in case one breaks." He strode past her and grabbed yet another flashlight.

Okay, this was ridiculous. She knew he took his job seriously, but his obsessive behavior teetered on the verge of some sort of manic breakdown.

She stepped between him and the shelves. He sucked in a sharp breath and met her gaze. "Aren't you going a bit overboard?"

"Not at all. Blueberry or raspberry?"

"What?"

"Which fruit bar do you prefer?" He looked past her left ear to boxes of food stacked on the shelf.

"Blueberry. But seriously, Ross. We aren't going to freeze, starve or need three sets of tire chains."

"You ever traveled the mountains in the winter? We could very well be stranded for up to a week if a storm hits."

"Did you check the weather? There's this thing called an app."

He grunted and reached around her to grab the box of blueberry fruit bars. "I know what I'm doing."

"I don't doubt you do—if you're heading a wagon train."

The light of his smirk danced in his eyes. "We don't want to have to resort to cannibalism."

He pivoted and headed to the truck. She watched him go, and even the sight of a gorgeous cowboy's backside in worn denim couldn't keep her from swaying with exhaustion.

After a whirlwind unboxing of her new wardrobe, thanks to Corrine, the woman made Pippa try it all on. She said there wasn't any point in keeping it if it didn't fit. But it had—every single thick sweater and soft flannel shirt, as well as three pairs of jeans, socks, boots, underwear and a heavy winter jacket with matching wool scarf, hat and gloves.

Pippa shopped online for clothes only when absolutely necessary, so to say she was overwhelmed received the award for understatement of the year. Everything had been packed away neatly into a canvas duffle bag with a heavy strap that Corrine had also purchased.

As if a full day at the lab, a death threat, fleeing to Montana and being swallowed by the Wyntons hadn't tired her out, watching Ross pack the truck as though they were headed into apocalypse territory did.

She followed him and leaned against the door. He finished stowing the blueberry bars, giving her a wonderful view of his strong back and the way his jeans hug nice and low on his—

She froze.

He carried a gun, tucked in the waist of his jeans along his spine.

At that moment, he straightened and looked at her hard. The realization came to her all over again—

she was on the run, from some crazy person who wanted to kill her. She wasn't in Montana to vacation and reunite with old friends. This old friend packed heat and would shoot to kill. She knew that as well as she knew he wouldn't stop packing the truck until he was satisfied they wouldn't perish on the road to Seattle.

"Pippa," he said in a soft drawl that sent shivers snaking up and down her spine. "You're dead on your feet. Maybe we should stay the night here. Leave in the morning."

She tipped her head, and her hair tumbled to the side like a waterfall. "You said yourself it's safer to travel at off times of day. I can steal a few hours of sleep in the truck."

Concern drew his brows together, and he searched her face. She had no doubt he could sniff out a lie clear across the Rockies. But he finally nodded.

"I'm finished here. Let's go in the house and say goodbye to my family."

The sun slanted lower in the sky, and she blinked against the glare. A sensation of this all being a dream amplified by the memory of following Ross around the ranch as a kid, waiting with stomach flutters for him to throw her a glance or smile.

So when he did that very thing, she felt too flustered to walk a straight line. Her shoulder bumped his, and he reached out to hook an arm around her middle. "God, you are dead on your feet,

Pip. Can you make it inside, or should I toss you over my shoulder?"

A vision of her rump high in the air, riding up around his head, planted two hot coals in her cheeks. She shook her head. "I'm fine."

To prove this, she pulled free of his touch before her fatigue made her do something stupid like fawn all over him. Quickening her pace, she made it to the house before he did.

He held the door for her. "Your legs are a lot longer than I remember."

Why did her stomach take a sharp dive at his comment? He was referring to something most humans had — legs. Some long, some short. No big deal. It wasn't as if he remarked on her breasts.

Oh God. Why did she have to think that?

Halfway to the house, Josiah and Noah intercepted Ross. He waved her on ahead, while he stopped to talk to them. She checked over her shoulder once and saw his shoulders set. All of them looked to be involved in a deep, serious discussion. About her?

The trio stood in the same stiff pose with steeled spines. Their white hats would give any girl a heart attack if she saw them headed her way.

A minute later, he jogged to catch up. Neither spoke as they continued to the house.

Saying farewell to the Wyntons always left her with pangs and bittersweet feelings. This time felt extra weighty, because she hardly spent any time with them.

But Mr. and Mrs. Wynton, along with Corrine, hugged her and Corrine even dropped a kiss to her cheek, surprising her with the display of affection. They hadn't been very close growing up, as so many years separated them. But now she couldn't resist kissing her cheek in return.

Then Ross, in true take-charge fashion, took her elbow and led her to the truck. In seconds, they were trundling down the driveway.

She looked at the house and barns and the beauty of it all. "I wish I could have stayed longer."

"You'll come back," he said with such conviction in his tone that she turned to him.

"Do you really believe that?"

He pierced her in his stare. "Yeah. I do. You're tired, Pippa. Don't get depressed on me. We have a lot of hours ahead of us."

She tossed a glance at the back seat piled with supplies and reached for one of the blankets. "Did we really need all this?"

"Never leave without enough to keep you warm and hydrated."

"What about the blueberry bars?"

"You'll be glad I brought them, believe me."

"Are you one of those men who never stops to eat, only for gas?"

"This truck has double gas tanks. It'll be a while." The corner of his mouth twitched, but he didn't dimple for her.

God, how she used to wish for that dimple. All the Wynton boys had one, but Ross's especially did things to her insides.

She draped the blanket over herself and the seat felt comfy enough, but her mind flitted like a wild bird did from branch to branch. The work she abandoned in the lab, things she planned to finish before leaving for Seattle, all left behind. She did have her laptop containing all her files, and the majority of her breakthrough experiment was burned into her brain, but her latest experiment was left behind.

"I wish I had all my data before I left the lab. Maybe I can access the database —"

"No." The single word sent goosebumps all over her body.

"Why not?"

"You can't contact the lab, even by accessing it through the internet. In fact, all emails go through me too."

At that instant, her cell phone buzzed. She sat forward to rummage in her computer bag for the device.

"Hand me the phone, Pippa." He held out a hand, broad palm up. The tone of his voice brooked no arguments.

She glanced at the screen. "It's only my friend Meredith!"

"Don't talk to her unless I'm on the line too."

"Don't be ridiculous. She's my friend from college!" Her voice ended on a rasp that reminded her of being choked what felt like days ago.

The phone buzzed again.

"I have to answer her, Ross." She started to accept the call, and he threw out a hand.

"Put it on speakerphone."

Seeing he wouldn't take anything less than her compliance, she answered and pressed speaker.

"Pippa! Thank goodness you picked up the phone. I was really worried when I saw you'd left early without signing out and then I couldn't reach you. What's going on?"

"Hi, Meredith. Thanks for checking up on me. I'm fine. Just had a sudden bout of sickness and left in a rush." She slanted a look at Ross, who responded with an approving nod.

"You do sound a little hoarse. Do you have a virus?"

"I think it might be influenza. I went home sick."

"How terrible. I'll stop in and bring you some soup."

Ross jerked a hand.

Fighting to keep the nerves from her tone, she said, "That's so sweet of you, Meredith, but I'd hate to think of passing these germs on to you."

Her friend sucked in a sharp gasp. "The conference! Will you be able to go? MIZR is relying on you to put our small lab on the map with your announcement."

"That's why I'm planning to rest a lot in the next couple days. I'm going to make that conference no matter what."

Ross gave a hard nod.

Annoyance rippled through her. She couldn't even take a phone call with an old friend without gaining his approval after every single word she said. He acted this way to keep her safe—because she asked him to. She couldn't get too angry with him, but did he need to be so highhanded?

"I'm glad you're still planning to attend. The whole world will be listening to you speak."

She winced. "Thanks for reminding me."

Meredith issued a light laugh. "Oh yeah...you get nervous being the center of attention."

"And you don't. Too bad we can't swap."

"I don't think anybody would mistake me for you, Pippa. Well, if you won't allow me to bring you soup, then please know I'm thinking about you. If you need a single thing—tissues, cold meds, lozenges, *anything*—just call and I'll be there."

Her heart warmed with her friend's sweet offer. "I appreciate it, Meredith. You're the best."

"Don't be silly. I know you'd do the same for me. Take care of yourself, Pippa."

The line went dead, and Pippa turned off her phone, feeling a little shaky at her lie.

"Quick thinking, telling her you're sick."

"I don't like lying, especially to friends."

"I doubt you've told many in your life. You were always a stickler for keeping to the rules."

"And you weren't. I remember you and your brothers used to try to get away with as much as you could. I always thought you did it to show off when my family was visiting."

"Nope. That was an everyday occurrence." He threw her a smile, dimple and all.

She stared at the divot in his cheek, feeling shakier but in a different way. He relaxed in the seat, one hand on the wheel as he sped them toward Seattle, and the pose only added to his appeal.

It was a silly thing, really, learning this strange new thing about herself. And at her age too.

Pippa studied him from the corner of her eye.

Who knew she liked a man who took charge?

Chapter Four

Ross avoided taking the turns in the highway too fast, and it wasn't due to road conditions.

No, every time he sped into a curve, Pippa's head would loll on the headrest into a more uncomfortable position as she slept.

Great—he'd become *that* person. One of those weirdos who wouldn't get up for fear of disturbing their cat/sleeping baby/any other innocent creature.

A low growl built in his throat, but again, he swallowed it because he didn't want to disturb her. The woman had endured so much already, and they had a long way to go before he got her safe.

Which led him to the other big issue—protecting her in a city, at a major conference, provided a whole new set of problems. He already had a call in to Boone to have him meet them as backup. And of course he'd get with security in the facility and double up. It still didn't ease his mind.

That call from her friend also itched at him. Meredith who? She'd fallen asleep before he could rifle more questions at her.

Night fell early at this time of year, the shadows on her face only broken by the glow coming from the dash lights. Under the shapeless wool blanket, he couldn't make out her figure.

Why was he trying to see her curves anyway? She might as well be a cousin to him. Yet as far from family as possible when it came to this strange twist in his gut.

He focused on his suspicions about Meredith. He needed Josiah to run the intel about the woman, and background checks on every employee at MIZR. He cast her a look. Talking on the phone would wake her.

Pippa's lack of worry or hesitation in her voice when she spoke to her friend told him she trusted Meredith—other than a slight hitch when she told her lie. He smiled to himself—she may not be the exact same girl he knew growing up, but her morals couldn't be shaken.

He wanted to trust her judgment concerning her friend. Pippa had a solid grip on common sense and she was smart. He knew those aspects of her personality. What he couldn't get over were the other changes that came from fifteen years of separation.

All traces of gawkiness had fled, leaving behind a timeless beauty, and though she was tall, her womanly curves were impossible to miss.

He glanced at her again. She'd removed her glasses and placed them in her bag by her feet. Seeing her without the eyewear create a tense knot in his core. A tumble of hair across her brow made him grip the wheel tighter to keep from reaching out to brush it away.

Whatever internal war waged inside him, he lacked time to deal with. He'd rarely lusted after a woman, and all his brothers razzed him for it. But he really didn't have time for the opposite sex. Dating required getting to know someone, spending time with her. Relationships tripled that time requirement, at least from what he saw with his baby brother, Noah.

He didn't really have a type, but if he did, he'd say she was an intellectual with a sense of humor — someone he could hold a conversation with and not want to drown her in the stock tank.

Christ, when she told him about her genetic discovery, he admittedly had a moment of dumbfounded awe for the woman. Then concern hit.

She'd put herself in the line of fire, her name in the spotlight. He believed somebody wanted to either steal her data or claim it as their own. Either way, Pippa was caught in the middle of a dangerous game.

Who the hell wanted her dead?

He couldn't help but feel they were staring down the barrel of a .45. Sure, he could defend them from attack while they drove — he trained extensively in evasive maneuvers, and the unmarked truck had been installed with bulletproof panels. Where he fell short right now was a lack of information.

Ross hated surprises. Ranchers dealt with them on a daily basis. A cow got sick. The market prices for beef fell out. Just because he dealt with surprises didn't mean he had to like them.

Pippa's breathing took on the slow, deep rhythm of a heavy sleep. If he was quiet, he could call Josiah. He withdrew his phone and hit a button with his thumb. Corrine's name immediately flashed on the screen, and he ended the call before she picked up.

He stifled a groan. Stupid big hands wouldn't work with small phone keyboards.

He got Josiah this time.

"Hey," he said quietly, slanting a look at Pippa. She slept on without rousing at the sound of his voice.

"You have a bad connection? You sound quiet."

"I'm trying not to wake Pippa."

"Gotcha. What do you need? You called at a bad time."

"Why? What's going on?" The muscles along his spine tightened.

"One of the ranch hands found a newborn calf dropped in the field."

"Jesus Christ. How the hell did one get impregnated so late?" They took care to keep their calves born in springtime. Montana winters were no good for calving.

"Who the hell knows. We missed one in the last pregnancy check, I guess."

"Is it alive?"

"Barely. The ranch hand got it into the saddle with him and wrapped in a blanket. He brought it back and placed her in the barn with heat lamps."

"Damn. Any sign of the momma?"

"Nope, and it's too dark to check right now. We're riding out at daybreak and search the herd for a cow that might be full of milk."

"It's not an ideal situation, but at least you found her." A lost calf cost the ranch enough money to make a difference in their bottom line, and the Wyntons didn't stay in the ranchin' business by losing money.

"Yeah, good thing. So what did you need? Because I know you didn't call about the calf."

Throwing Pippa another glance to make sure she was still asleep, he said, "Get me a list of all the employees working at MIZR. I want backgrounds on every person including their families."

"MIZR's a big company. This is gonna take me some time."

"Rope Corrine into helping. She's good at following directions."

"Okay. I did find something you might find important."

"What's that?" The edge to his voice stirred Pippa.

She shifted in the seat, drew the blanket up over her shoulders and slept on.

"I gave you a bad route to follow."

"Are you fucking serious? I can't be off course. I know I'm headed west." Though he had a good sense of direction, he swept the road illuminated by his headlights for road signs.

"Not the wrong route—there's a storm blowing in from the north."

"You didn't check the weather before sending us this way?"

"Give me a little credit, would ya, Ross? Of course I checked. The storm was supposed to blow southeast but some stupid pressure system's turned it west instead."

"Great. What am I lookin' at?"

"Heavy snow."

"I got chains."

"Ice."

"Still covered."

"High winds."

"I've got enough supplies to keep us going for a few days."

"You can always go southwest and then turn north."

"I will if necessary, but I might not get to Seattle in time if we do. Thanks for the head's up, Josiah."

"You got it. Anything else?"

"I'll check in about the calf in the morning. Run those backgrounds for me, will ya?"

"You nag a hell of a lot. Anybody ever tell you that?"

"Yeah," he said with a quirk of his lips, "you do every damn day."

After ending the call, Ross looked over at Pippa again. Her head turned enough to see the peace of slumber on her face. Seeing her this way, completely vulnerable...

He twisted his attention to the windshield again. The headlights caught on the first flakes of snow whirling in the wind. They were headed into a storm.

And in the mountains, they had a hell of a good chance of being stranded.

Worse — they'd be stranded alone, with no one to stop him from acting on his urge to pull her flush against him and plunder her sweet, full lips.

Ten minutes down the road, data started to flood in, and his phone beeped with emails. The snow fell faster and thicker. He rerouted his GPS, but the first chance to turn south was in forty miles. The weather could make that journey turn into hours.

He wanted to stop and read through some of the information Josiah — and probably Corrine — sent, but he couldn't stop now.

He uncapped a bottle of water and drank the entire thing. Without thinking, he tossed the empty bottle over the seat. The crinkly sound of the plastic hitting one of the spare sets of chains on the floor made Pippa sit up straight.

She looked around in confusion, her gaze landing on him.

"Ross."

Whenever he heard her gritty tone – he now knew as a result of her attack – he wanted to snap someone's neck.

"It's okay. We're on the road."

She blinked at the windshield and then reached for her glasses. Once they were on her face, she said, "I thought it was snowing."

"Can't you tell without your glasses?"

"I can see blobs. Colors. That's about all."

"Why don't you get that laser eye surgery?"

"I might someday. I've been a little busy the past decade."

"Busy finding breakthroughs that will change medicine."

She tucked her chin into the blanket and grew quiet for a long minute. He'd embarrassed her – and it was the cutest damn thing he'd ever seen. He wished the sun was up so he could see her complexion. Did her blood draw to the surface of her skin? Did her flush make her freckles stand out?

"Should it be snowing so much?" she changed the topic.

"Well, it is late fall. That means snow in the mountains, and we're heading into it. Worse, Josiah just told me they found a newborn calf on the ranch."

"Oh no." She brushed that lock of hair away. "You weren't expecting it to be born now?"

"We don't calve in fall. We like them to be born when it's warmer and no chance of them dropping in the snow, like this one did."

"Will it be okay?" The dash lights reflected off the lenses of her glasses, but he saw her eyes were wide with worry.

He didn't consciously plan to reach out and touch her arm.

His hand just sort of ended up there.

She stilled under his touch. The wool blanket had a rougher feel than he knew the skin under it would be. Still, she wore several layers as barrier between his flesh and hers.

For the better.

He pulled back and clenched his hand on his thigh. "Do you like working for MIZR?"

Before answering, she unbuckled her seatbelt and leaned over the console to locate something in the back seat. He gritted his teeth at the sight of her round ass in the air.

A second later she dropped into her seat with a bottle of water and the box of blueberry bars. She drank and ate the bar, taking her good old time before answering his question.

When she crumpled the empty wrapper and tucked it into the pocket on the door, she offered him the box.

He waved a hand.

"You don't like blueberry?"

"I'm good."

She pulled a second from the box and ate it too. Just when he thought he'd go crazy waiting for her response, she broke the silence. "I love my company. They recruited me when I was in high school."

"You're kidding me."

The note of shyness seeped into her tone. "I won a science competition. And it got some notice."

"I'm surprised my parents never said anything about it."

"MIZR granted me a scholarship to attend Yale, to be doubled if I signed a three-year contract with them."

"So you're locked in."

She shook her head. "No. I fulfilled the terms of that contract and stayed on with them."

"I see."

"To be honest, Ross, I'd be shocked to learn someone in the lab threatened me. We're sort of a family. We throw geeky parties roasting marshmallows over Bunsen burners."

He huffed a laugh. "We did that in high school."

"Yes, we are just as nerdy as you'd expect scientists working in a lab to be. I don't know a single person who would want to hurt me."

He heard the pain echo in her voice, and he got that pang again—the urge to reach out and soothe her. To protect.

To kill for her.

Goddamn, he was in trouble.

* * * * *

When Pippa emerged from the skanky truck stop restroom, a set of wide shoulders loomed up. She shrank with a scream bottled in her throat.

Then instinct kicked in.

Her elbow drew back, and she aimed all her force at the man's jaw.

The blow connected, and pain shot up her arm.

"What the...?" The man grappled with her, and she aimed another blow, this one for the bridge of his nose.

"Stop! Fucking hell, Pip! It's me—Ross!" He grabbed her shoulders.

Shock rippled through her. She'd just delivered an elbow strike to her bodyguard. Irritation followed hard on the heels of her shock.

"Why are you lurking outside the bathroom door? You scared the fudge out of me."

"Don't you ever swear?"

She gaped at him. "What?"

He rubbed at his jaw. "C'mon, say it, Pippa—you scared the fuck outta me, Ross." He took her by the

70

arm and led her across the pavement to the truck parked a short distance away. The bright lights and rumble of diesel engines, along with the thickly falling snow, lent a surreal feeling to the night. As if she needed her life to feel like more of a dream.

As soon as they were settled in the locked truck, she drew the blanket over herself.

His green eyes were cast in shadow by his hat. "Are you going to say it or not?"

"No, I'm not."

"C'mon, Pippa."

"Are we kids again and you're trying to pressure me into saying a bad word so we both get in trouble?"

His lips twitched at the corner. "It will make you feel better."

"Is this some kind of 'bellow to the world how you're feeling so you get it off your chest' moment?"

"Exactly."

"And you were trained in the psychology of this?"

"Not exactly."

"Then why do you want me to say the F word?"

He dropped his gaze to her lips. "You don't have to say it. We'd best get on the road. And to answer your question, I waited for you outside the restroom to make sure you weren't attacked again."

Her stomach knotted. "Well...thank you."

"Doin' my job."

71

"What do you charge for your services anyway? What's the going rate for a bodyguard?"

"Personal protection officers receive about a thousand bucks a week. But our prices are a bit on the higher end, due to our training and reputation."

"How *did* you manage to build your company so quickly?"

"How did you make the discovery of the century?" he turned the tables on her.

She tugged the blanket up to her chin. "Hard work and a little luck."

His teeth flashed. "Same here."

He focused on the road. Heavy snow drifted across the asphalt, driven by the winds that rocked the truck. She knotted her fingers in her lap.

"Crap." He peered through the windshield.

"What is it?"

"Detour. They must have the road closed ahead."

The man must have superhero vision, because all she saw was a whiteout. "Is this safe? Should we stop somewhere for the night?"

"We're in the Rockies, sweetheart. We're going to be up here a while. Don't worry, I've driven this pass before, and it's very safe. Things at night can look a little spooky."

"If by spooky you mean there's a terrifying million-foot drop on my side of the road, then yes."

"Trust me. I'll get you to Seattle in one piece."

She reached for another blueberry bar and ate it in four bites. The Wyntons had given her a lovely family dinner before they left, but years of late-night cramming sessions in college turned her into a snacker. She found nibbling on something during the night kept her more alert. Maybe it was the sugar rush.

Ross geared down and then slowed more to pull off the road into a wide spot. He put the truck in park.

"What are you doing?"

"Putting chains on."

"Oh. Do you need help?"

He shrugged into his coat, which he drove without while she sat bundled beneath a blanket. "I can manage alone, but if you'd like to see how it's done, grab your hat and gloves."

She'd never need to put chains on her own tires, as she had no plans to cross the Rockies alone in the future. But she disliked being helpless, so she slipped on her hat and gloves and followed him outside.

The wind hit her like an icy wall. She braced herself against it for a moment, instantly shaking with cold. She couldn't even hear the clink of the chains Ross removed from the truck.

When she rounded to his side, she found him squatting by the rear tire draping the chains over the rubber. She squatted next to him and screamed to be heard above the howl of the wind. "Why didn't we do this earlier at the truck stop?"

"Wasn't sure what we'd get into, and I have good tires. We'll make it without the chains, but this will make our drive a bit easier."

She watched his quick, easy movements as he applied the chains the way he did everything on the ranch, with a natural ability she was always impressed with. As a girl, she loved watching Ross saddle a horse, and once she'd stood at the fence watching him break a yearling. Her girlish heart pounded out of her chest.

Now parts other than her heart were affected by his closeness and the manly work.

He looked at her, hat pulled down against the wind. "Can you get behind the wheel and drive forward a little? A slow roll forward, enough to get the chain in a position to link it on the backside."

She nodded. Anything to get out of this snow and wind.

She jogged forward and jumped in the truck. Snow coated the windshield, and she had to switch on the wipers before she could see to roll forward even an inch. She didn't want to take a chance she'd drive off the ledge.

A shiver rolled through her, and she set her teeth in her lip as she put the truck in gear and slowly crept forward. After she stopped, she opened the door to look back at Ross. He waved her ahead a little more. Then he gestured for her to stop, and she hopped out again to watch how he clipped the chains and then tightened them using a long metal bar.

They did the same for the other three tires and when she settled in the heated truck under her wool blanket again, she couldn't be more grateful for the warmth and comfort of the vehicle.

While he drove, the silence made her sleepy. She switched on the radio and found nothing but static.

"Even satellite radio isn't working in this storm," he told her.

"What about cell service?" She grabbed her phone but Ross was right that everything had been knocked out by the storm and the mountains blocking signals at this elevation didn't help.

"Nothing." She dropped her phone into her bag again and downed another blueberry bar to keep her attention from wandering to his big hands. He'd removed his heavy leather gloves and his long fingers latched around the leather wheel.

Even with the flavor of blueberry in her mouth, she could almost taste the man who sat a foot away from her. He'd taste like he smelled—musky with a clean hint of soap.

Her gaze dropped to his hands again. The backs of his knuckles were lightly dusted with dark hair and veins snaked upward to disappear into the cuffs of his shirt, as he'd removed his jacket again.

A new kind of shiver ran through her from head to toe—a need to feel those big, capable, rough hands on her.

The truck slowed to a crawl through the deepening snow. Wind rocked the vehicle. Soon they were traveling so slow that she hardly felt them moving at all.

"Ross, do you think we should stop? We're not making any progress."

His mouth tightened, which created a bracket in his cheek. "I was thinkin' the same. The thought of stopping doesn't set well with me, but it might be best. We've got plenty of gas to keep the truck running and warm. As soon as the sun comes over those mountains in a few hours, we'll have better visibility."

"Plus, you've got to be exhausted."

When he turned his head, she saw no trace of fatigue lining his face. Instead, some other emotion lived in his eyes.

Something that had her insides trembling.

"Pretty sure the pass widens up ahead. I'll find a safe spot to pull off and we'll wait out the storm. I could kick Josiah's ass for giving me this route."

"Why is it Josiah's fault?"

"He's our details guy. He does most of our research and gets us from point A to B."

"And he failed to be a meteorologist too, I guess."

He huffed a breath through his nose. "That's right."

Long minutes later and a few miles down the road, Ross located a place off to the side to pull over.

He parked and within minutes the windshield grew covered with snow, leaving her with a feeling of being buried alive.

She issued a low sigh. "I'm sorry for being so much trouble, Ross."

Across the expanse of the truck, he looked at her hard. "I told you it's my job, Pippa."

"I don't want to be a job," she rasped in a whisper.

His throat made a noise as he swallowed. "You've had a hard few days. Let's talk."

"What do you want to talk about?" She angled in the seat to face him.

"Tell me your hopes and dreams. Your goals."

She smiled. "We really are diving back in time. I want to be a soccer star and doctor in some warm climate and you want to run a horse ranch and fight fires part time."

His deep, rumbling chuckle provided instant heat to the truck cab. "I forgot about that talk we had with my brothers and your little sister on the patio. Seems like a thousand years ago."

Her insides clenched in an unmistakable display of arousal. Of all times to be turned on—on a mountain during a blizzard, stuck inches away from her childhood crush.

"You don't run a horse ranch or fight fires," she said.

"And you aren't a soccer star, unless you haven't given me the whole story."

She gave a throaty laugh. "No. That dream died when my legs got too long for me to control them."

He eyed her. "Seems as if you figured it out."

Why did his tone and the glimmer in his eyes make her want to wiggle in her seat? No, more than wiggle—strip off her clothes and invite him under her blanket with her.

She shivered.

"Maybe you should climb in the back seat and sleep."

"You're just as tired as I am." Now visions of both of them tangled up, her thighs around his hips and his mouth moving over hers, blasted her mind like the wintry wind.

He gazed at his hands for a minute, fisted on his lap. Her stomach plummeted—could he be thinking the same things she was?

Impossible. Though she didn't consider herself bad looking, she wouldn't win any prizes for beauty. Besides, Ross didn't see her that way.

"If I cut the engine, the cab will stay warm about an hour." He spoke in slow syllables as though measuring their meaning.

She held her breath.

Another minute passed.

He turned his head and pierced her in his stare. "I'll climb in the back and you follow, Pippa."

Her stomach fluttered uncontrollably. He set his hat on the center console and then opened the door. Wind rushed in, and she gasped at the icy blast before he slammed the door. A moment passed. Several, in fact. What was taking him so long? Had he slipped and fallen on the roadside?

She was about to get out and check, when he opened the back door and settled inside.

Twisting in her seat, she met his stare. Snow lay on his shoulders and created sparkles on his white hat.

A heavy beat hung between them.

Then she did what she really wanted to and climbed over the console, dragging her blanket with her.

Ross grabbed her hips and eased her to the seat next to him. She had to curl her legs to keep her boots off the water and other supplies. For a moment, her innate awkwardness took control, and she sat stiff on the seat.

Until he shifted around to stretch his legs and propped his boots on the case of water.

"Here, you'll fit in this space next to me." He patted the seat.

She'd be wedged between the leather and his big, hot, muscled, good-smelling body.

Right where she wanted to be.

Drawing a deep breath, she squeezed in beside him. Her back rested against his chest—he took up too much room to give her much.

"How are you so warm?"

He chuckled and reached for the blanket, tucking it around her. "I'm hot-blooded."

His statement made her own blood run ten degrees warmer and warmth slipped low between her thighs.

A long minute passed with nothing but the thud of her own heart.

Chapter Five

Don't get out of the seat, he'd told himself.

Sitting at that wheel became a battle complete with the clash of steel will against steely need.

If he climbed in the back of the truck with Pippa, he didn't know if it'd be possible to hold back.

He had to hold back. He'd sit here till dawn, till the storm broke, till hell froze over, but he wouldn't get out of the truck.

In the end, he got out.

Then he stood in the howling fucking gale force wind with snow and ice pelting him, dragging in deep breaths and fighting the strongest urges of his life.

Now she pressed against his side, warm and soft with her curves giving him balls so blue they might as well have frostbite.

Worst goddamn idea of his life. But at least Pippa was warm.

She also smelled like blueberries and honey and apple blossoms.

Getting her scent out of his nose proved impossible with her snuggled up like a sweet kitten. Her shivering stopped and her muscles relaxed, sinking bit by bit into him.

"Ross?"

"Hmm?"

Christ, her voice drove him crazy. He wanted to heal the rasp, but it threaded through him and left him aching.

"Do you think we're being followed?" The question came out with a quiver, like a child voicing her fears in the dark after she heard a noise.

He slid his arm around her and drew her closer to him. "No." The word rumbled past her ear he wanted to suck and nibble until she gasped. "And if they were, let's hope they're more unprepared than we are."

When she nodded, her head rubbed on his shoulder.

"When was the last time you saw your family?" He aimed his question to take her mind off their immediate troubles of being stopped by the storm, huddled together in the back seat, and now the more disturbing fact that his cock was starting to swell.

"Thanksgiving."

"Nearly a year."

"My mom reminds me of that often enough."

"It can't be easy, living clear across the country without family."

"I do miss them a lot. I actually heard about your company at Thanksgiving."

He pictured the Hamlins sitting down to dinner together, the table set for four including her sister Holly, and the topic of his business venture coming up.

"That's how you knew to call me." Everything made sense now.

She lapsed into silence for several minutes. He knew she wasn't sleeping by the energy that seemed to flow through her body. He swore he could hear her brain whirring. He definitely heard the snow falling, shrouding the truck.

"I have to admit you surprised me with your martial arts skills. My jaw still hurts. I think you bruised it."

She twisted in his hold to peer at him as if she could see through the darkness. He studied her eyes a moment before she dropped them to his jaw. "I can't see anything with your five o'clock shadow."

Her voice sounded throatier than before, and he ground his teeth against a dark clutch of desire.

He only needed a second to have her stretched out on top of him and his mouth on hers. But there would be no turning back from such an act. No more innocent, easygoing banter at family barbecues. No more fly fishing without a hell of a lot of tension underscoring every interaction.

Hands off, Wynton.

Did that mean lips off too? How about his cock?

Pippa's off-limits.

"Ross?" Her voice sent another shock of need to his groin.

"Yeah?"

"You scared the fuck outta me at that truck stop."

A smile spread slowly over his face, until he felt his eyes crease with it. God, she could drive a man crazy. Her drawl a perfect imitation of his.

His chuckle pulled a soft giggle from her too. The closeness he felt in that minute... It rocked him.

He started to reach toward her face — to cup it and pull her lips to his.

Something vibrated against his thigh, jolting him back to his senses just in time.

"It's your phone," she said.

Shifting to remove the device from his pocket without her seeing his bulging erection proved to be a challenge. He brought his phone to his ear on the third buzz.

"Ross."

"Hey. The storm looks bad on the radar. Where ya at?"

"We had to pull off. We weren't making any progress. It's a whiteout."

"So you're just parked along the mountain?"

"Pretty much. Did you call to give me a weather update?"

Pippa turned her head at his rough tone.

"No, a calf update."

He waited to hear they'd lost it.

"Dad and Corrine got it warmed up and managed to get some milk into it. It's hangin' on. The storm's heading our way, so the ranch hands went out with lights to track down the momma and bring her back. Such a lot of trouble for a calf."

"But it's our responsibility."

"You're preachin' to the choir, Ross. I was raised a rancher too. Now, about the information you need. Did you get a chance to read over those emails?"

"Not yet. I was driving."

"Well what are you doing now?"

Ross hoped to hell Pippa couldn't hear Josiah speaking, but she sat close enough, practically in his lap, that he wouldn't be surprised if she could. How to respond to his brother? Tell him he and Pippa were curled up together in the back seat?

"I'll get to the emails."

Pippa gave him the side-eye.

"Thanks, Josiah," he added so he wouldn't sound like a complete ass.

"I'm surprised I got you on the phone. I called four times."

He hadn't thought of it when his phone rang. "Service is spotty. You must have caught a signal between snowflakes. If you don't hear from me, don't send out a search party for at least a couple days."

A smile leaked into his brother's voice. "You think I give a damn about your ass freezing in the Rockies?"

Pippa's smile told Ross that she could, in fact, hear.

"Bye, dickhead."

"Bye, you old fuck."

He ended the call and slipped his phone into the pocket on the back of the driver's seat.

"Why did Josiah call you an old fuck?"

He damn near groaned. Hearing the prim little rule-follower scientist cuss twice in the same hour made his attraction to her spike.

"He thinks I'm older than my years."

She grew quiet, but he was getting used to these spells. In fact, they were growing on him. He was the first to admit he liked to talk. Discussing every small detail of the ranch and protection company came as second nature to him. While he might be extroverted in this manner, Pippa was not.

Isolated in the middle of a blizzard with the woman gave him a new respect for her. He also felt an urge to extract every single secret from her.

Such as did she date? What was her type?

And did she slide her fingers into her pussy at night and pleasure herself?

She snapped her head to look at him. "Am I crushing you? I can move to the other end of the seat."

Confusion pinched his brows. "No, why?"

"You groaned."

Fuck, did he?

"Just thinking of that calf is all."

"I'm sure it's worrisome, being away from the ranch. I'm sorry I dragged you off."

This time he couldn't resist cupping her cheek and tilting her head to meet his gaze. Christ, her skin was silky and more tender than he imagined.

"Pippa, let's get it straight now that you needing help is not something to apologize for. Even if I didn't work as a protection officer, I'd still help you. Got that?"

Her eyelids fluttered. For a moment, he thought he'd gone too far, been too harsh with her. As a young girl, she'd run off to the house with a red face whenever he or his brothers took the teasing too far.

But then she tipped her head against his palm and shut her eyes.

His heart slammed his ribs as he cradled her face, staring at the peaceful expression she wore. In the darkness, he couldn't make out her freckles. And he wanted to see them up close.

Instead... He stared at her lips, a plump shadow of enticement and torture. His balls clenched.

He never realized he was moving in to kiss her until her eyes popped open and she pulled free.

Dropping his hand, he fought to cover the moment. He grabbed his hat and stuffed it down on his head again, centering the brim low on his eyes. "You should get what sleep you can, Pippa. I'll start the truck in a little bit and warm it back up."

She snuggled against his shoulder once more. "I'm warm."

Fuck.

No way in hell could he sleep, so he flipped through the emails. After reading through information on several of her coworkers, and seeing the same boring lives over and over, he had to wonder how a woman with a mind like Pippa's managed to work with such duds. She must find herself yawning her way through conversations at the water cooler—unless they stood around discussing gene editing.

Which they might. He and his family talked ranch life, didn't they? Hell, at the last bonfire a few weeks back, he and the employees of WEST Protection kicked back with beers and talked over their cases long into the night.

He was a dud too, it seemed. Older than his time for damn sure.

He flipped to an email with an in-depth look at MIZR and all the executives of the board. He followed the trails down rabbit hole after rabbit hole, until he knew whose wife had slept with which director and who wintered in the Caribbean. What he didn't find was a single person with a motive.

Nobody with ties to another company looking to steal Pippa's research. He shot off a text to his brother to send someone to start interrogating the staff at the lab.

"Don't you ever sleep?" Pippa's question broke through his thoughts.

He offered a tip of his lips in a gentle smile. "Speak for yourself, Hamlin."

She gave him a full smile in return. "What are you doing on your phone? I know you're not crushing candy."

He grunted with amusement. "I'm investigating your workplace and everybody in it."

When she sat up straighter, her thigh brushed the length of his, shooting sparks of fire through every inch of his body. Just when he thought he was finished being aroused by his family friend, she did a small thing like *move*.

"Did you find anything about them?"

"No. That's why I'm sending one of our team to question them."

Her mouth fell open into a perfect O...and he refused to think about what would fit inside that opening.

Fuck, he just did.

She wet her lips, making his pain worse.

"Won't that alert whoever it is that we're on to them?"

"Exactly. People slip up more when they get scared."

She leaned forward, dropping her face into her hands. She scrubbed them over her face and raked her fingers through her hair, freeing the scent that'd been driving him crazy all day. Two days? Hell, he'd lost track.

All he knew was if he sat here with her much longer, he couldn't account for his actions.

He reached behind him for the door handle. "Time to start the truck."

* * * * *

Pippa swallowed down another blueberry bar and then extended her cold fingers toward the heating vents. Ross had the engine running and the heat blasting while he cleared the snow off the truck.

The long hours of the night provided little sleep but strangely she didn't mind the exhaustion.

Maybe it was sugar rushing through her veins...or time spent with Ross.

She wished her girlhood crush hadn't risen from the depths of her soul to torment her, but she liked him more than ever. After she was safe and they parted ways, she'd have to wait another decade before seeing him again or risk making an ass of herself.

Everything about the man appealed to her from the way he wore his Stetson pulled low over his eyes to the way he drawled certain words. And don't get her started about that moment when he'd cupped her face.

She couldn't make out his reason for doing such a thing, and her insides still fluttered from the impact of the look in his eyes.

When she reached for the box of blueberry bars again, she found a lone bar in the bottom. She started to unwrap it and drew it to her lips. Ross opened the driver's door and wind blasted in.

He glanced at the bar in her hand. "Got one for me?"

She swallowed hard. "Uh…this is the last one."

Dropping into the seat, he slammed the door and stared at her. "You ate the whole box?"

"It was a small box."

"But you ate them all."

"You said staying hydrated is most important." She knew she wasn't making sense, and her argument was trash.

His eyes widened, and the green depths burned her to the seat. An inferno rushed into her belly and settled between her thighs.

"Gimme a bite." The command came off with those drawled syllables she'd started asking herself if she could live without.

She held the bar out of his reach.

Or so she thought.

Ross had long arms — long enough to swipe out a hand and pluck the bar from her fingers. A squeak of surprise escaped her as she watched him bring it to his lips.

Either hunger kicked in or an extreme sense of competition. She threw herself at him. He moved the bar, but not in time — she closed her jaws over it, ripping off the top half.

"You little..." He gaped at her in shock while she chewed. He was so distracted that hardly an eyelash flickered as she took the bar from his hand and stuffed the rest in her mouth.

Jaw gaping, he shook his head. "Who knew you'd ever battle a man for the last blueberry bar?"

"I was hungry. You don't want to see me when I get beyond hungry. It's not pretty." She offered him a smile but that fell away as he lunged for her again.

He trapped her against the passenger door with his big body looming over hers. A wall of heat and strength pressed her down. When he looked into her eyes, she sucked in a breath.

In a swift move, he stamped his lips on hers.

It wasn't a quick, chaste peck but a hard demand of his lips. Need flooded her. She started to gasp, but he withdrew two inches, still staring at her.

"Wh...what was that for?" she whispered.

His eyes creased in a smile. "I at least wanted a taste."

92

He plopped into his seat again and gripped the wheel. During the night, a plow had cleared some of the snow on the road, and while flakes still fell fast, they were smaller and the wind wasn't blowing as much.

As they pulled onto the road, she gaped at what Ross had just done. Wanted a taste? Of the blueberry...or of her?

The latter had her core coiling with desire and her pussy squeezed in response.

After all these years of crushing on Ross Wynton, she'd finally gotten her kiss.

Staring at him for several miles didn't offer her any clues as to why he'd done it. She wished she knew what was going on in his head.

If she had another bar, she'd tempt him a second time.

Being on the road for the umpteenth hour reminded her how grungy she felt. She hadn't brushed her teeth. And squatting on the roadside to relieve herself after 'staying hydrated' didn't count as using a bathroom.

"How far until the next stop?"

"Twenty miles or so. There's a gas station at the bottom of the mountain." He tossed her a look. "You still hungry?"

"I might be." Though she'd never been sassy in her life, Ross drew it out of her.

His dimple was her reward. As was the tingle lingering in her lips from his kiss.

She analyzed the shocking caress for the entire ride, replaying it over and over and wondering if she'd reacted in a way that put him off or egged him on.

By the time she spotted the stop with a gas station and diner, relief struck that she could spend a few minutes away from Ross. He plucked at her nerves — heartstrings too — until she chimed with a melody of confusion and desire, neither of which she knew how to handle in such close proximity to the cowboy bodyguard.

"I'm surprised so many people are out today." She pointed to the full parking lot.

He slowed but stopped short of the commitment to turn in.

"Aren't we stopping?"

"I don't like the crowd there."

The road zipped by. "Well, how far until the next stop?"

"Two hours barring we don't hit more bad weather."

The thought of waiting two more hours for a real restroom facility where she could wash her face and brush her teeth made her groan internally.

"I'm sure it's safe. Nobody attacked us back at the last truck stop."

"You attacked me," he said.

"Because you were skulking around the bathroom door!"

"First you said I was lurking. Now I'm skulking. If you really need to stop, wait 'til you see the level of protection I provide in this place."

What had she gotten herself into?

He parked at the end, farther from all the other trucks and SUVs in the lot. She started to get out, and he told her to wait.

So she sat there like a child waiting for her parent to come unbuckle her from the car seat. When he opened her door and helped her down, she discovered just how stiff her muscles were from being cramped in a truck all night.

"Okay?" He took her elbow.

She nodded. "I just need to stretch my legs."

Two people exited the convenience store, and he reached around his back. A shiver of awareness took hold of her—he carried a weapon.

He led her the long way around the lot, which gave her a chance to walk the stiffness out of her legs, but she got a feeling he was doing it to keep her safe.

When they located the restroom, fear suddenly surged inside her. She stared at the closed door.

Ross placed his mouth to her ear. "You don't think I'm going to let you go in alone, do you?" After dropping that bombshell, he shoved the door open and swept a look over the room like one of those cops she saw on TV.

One other stall door was closed and the tinkling sound of the woman peeing reached Pippa.

"You can't come in," she whispered hotly. "It's an invasion of privacy!"

"Your safety comes first."

She'd been attacked in a restroom in a crowded public place. Maybe Ross was right. She didn't relish the thought of someone coming at her again.

He remained frozen to his spot. It was either use the facilities with him standing there or go along the roadside again, this time with cars driving past.

She looked him in the eye. He arched a brow.

In a huff, she whirled and strode to the stall. She slammed it a little too hard and locked it. When she heard the other woman in the restroom issue an exclamation, she knew she'd encountered Ross.

"Pervert!"

Pippa heard a thump and her heart rocketed into her throat. Then she heard Ross drawl, "Ma'am."

Pippa could just see him thumbing the brim of his hat and offering his dimpled Wynton charm to the poor woman as she washed her hands and scurried out.

Pippa hovered over the seat.

Long seconds passed.

"Ross."

"What's wrong?"

"I can't...*go*...with you standing there listening."

"Well, I'm not leaving. How 'bout this?" A hand dryer roared to life. Then another and another.

Seconds later, she emerged from the stall, and she ducked her head to hide the heat in her face. He watched her as she washed her hands and waited while she dried them.

So much for changing her clothes. Or brushing her teeth. She'd have to do that in the parking lot with a bottle of water.

She slanted a look at him. "That was uncomfortable."

"But you're safe."

She couldn't argue with that fact.

"What did that lady hit you with?"

"Her purse." Amusement teased his lips.

She bit back a smile as they left the restroom with him acting like a wolf guarding his dinner from the rest of the pack as they approached the food counter.

She hated that she'd lost her purse. She'd never gotten around to setting up an electronic wallet to pay on her cell phone, and now she regretted it because the menu boasted a big, juicy burger that her mouth watered for.

Peeing with Ross within earshot was embarrassing, but not as embarrassing as having no money and wanting a burger.

He took her arm in a protective hold and led her to the clerk. "Two o' those loaded burgers."

97

Pippa blinked. How did he know she was craving that burger?

"Everything on them?" the kid at the register asked.

"Yup. Fries too. And two o' those apple pies."

Her stomach burned with hunger that even an entire box of blueberry bars couldn't touch.

"To go," Ross added and paid with cash.

She noted how he kept tabs on every person surrounding them. Also, how he angled his body in a certain fashion...like he was prepared to take a bullet for her.

She stared at his handsome profile, focused on his hard lips and remembering the feel of them on hers.

When they had the food bag in hand and started across the parking lot, Ross tossed several looks behind him.

"You're making me edgy. Why are you looking around like that?"

"Just have a feeling is all."

"A *feeling*?" Her boot slipped on some ice and she almost face-planted, but he caught her and pulled her into his side.

Something bit her leg. Or stung it.

She screamed in surprise even as her mind landed on the fact it was winter and all the bees were hibernating. In the parking lot, other people screamed. She heard an engine rev as though gearing up to escape.

Next thing she knew, she was in Ross's arms. His boots thudded on the icy pavement and he shoved her between two vehicles.

"What the—" she started to say and then saw his reason for spiriting her away.

Two tall men in black wearing black ski masks to conceal their identity came at them, one with a weapon raised.

The pain in her calf—that sting—had come from a bullet.

She'd been shot.

She couldn't glance away from Ross to check the sticky blood she felt on her leg. One man ran forward, and the other fired on them.

A shriek bottled in her throat. Her head spun with terror that froze her in place as if a winter king had prodded her with his fingertip and stopped her in her tracks.

She couldn't let Ross handle two men at once.

With a war cry, she threw herself forward. But her injured leg couldn't launch her into the jumping strike she intended to snap her attacker's neck.

She crumpled to the ground, barely catching herself before her cheek hit the ice. Ross shoved her behind him as he tore his weapon from the waist of his jeans. His shot rang out.

A thump sounded, and a man fell feet from her. Blood bloomed on the ice, but his staring eyes told her all she needed to know.

Ross struck the second attacker with a swing of his fist. When he slammed into the frozen pavement, she checked her scream of horror. More thudding noises landed in her ears as Ross pummeled the man on the ground next to her.

She clawed her way to a sitting position. Breathing hard and fast, she used the SUV beside her to pull herself up. A haze of shock froze her in place, the only things registering were Ross's grunts and the thump of his fists against flesh. She stared at Ross's back as he delivered blow after blow to the man on the ground.

"Ross!" She stumbled forward. "Stop!"

His ski mask had peeled back to reveal most of his slack face.

"He's unconscious!"

Ross grunted and then kicked him one more time with enough strength to ensure the man urinated blood for a month. Then panting, fists curled, he turned to look at her.

She balanced on her good leg, chest heaving.

Ross's eyes still blazed with fury, and in that strangely still second, with snowflakes swirling around them, she saw everything the man was capable of.

Chapter Six

Rule number one: Always have an escape plan.

Don't engage in a shootout and leave your ward unguarded was a close second.

He'd broken both rules.

And worse, he'd kissed her. He might as well turn the company over to Boone to run and Ross could return to something he was actually good at—ranching.

"What do we do?" Pippa's hot whisper reverberated with terror.

"I've got plastic in the back of the truck."

Her eyes flared wide. "You can't be serious! We can't take them with us! You have to call the police!"

He knew she was right. But he was still staring through a red haze that marred the snowy white world with his rage. His pulse hammered with it. His stomach clenched with it. He would kill every single man who came after Pippa, and he'd fight dirty.

"Ross!" She stumbled toward him, and he dropped his gaze to her calf. Blood soaked her jeans in a dark stain.

His fury retreated enough for his training to kick in again. Leaving the bodies for travelers to come across wasn't ideal, but getting Pippa safe came first.

He lifted her and ran to the truck, swinging his head right and left and tossing glances over each shoulder. He got her into the truck and met her gaze.

"I'm going to cut open the hole in your jeans and look at your wound."

She bit down on her lip but nodded.

After pulling out his pocketknife, he sliced the denim. His balls shriveled at the sight of the deep gouge in her leg—then relief flooded in that the bullet only nicked her.

"The bullet just grazed you. You're bleeding a lot, but it's starting to clot already. Are you okay for the moment?"

She slumped in the seat, head in her hands. "Yes."

Jumping behind the wheel, he tossed her his phone and told her his passcode. "Call Josiah and tell him what happened. Tell him to get the state police here immediately and inform him we're getting back on the highway."

"We're getting back on the highway?" Her voice pitched higher with every word.

He backed out of the parking space and all the way across the lot to where the attackers lay. One still breathed, though Ross had made damn sure he'd never reproduce.

He reached across her and popped the glove compartment, locating a burner phone. "Stay here. Don't unlock the doors. If you hear anything, do not get out. You hear me, Pippa?" His cutting tone gave him what he needed from her — a nod of agreement.

He jumped out and locked her in. With phone in hand, he snapped photos of each man and shot them off to Josiah.

He climbed behind the wheel again and drove as fast as conditions would allow, the urge to put miles between them and her attackers a coal burning in the hollow of his gut.

"Are you okay?" He threw her a look.

Her hazel eyes were frantic. "We can't just…drive away! Ross, you killed that man! The other might be dying!"

"The police are on the way."

"But you're fleeing the scene!"

"I've got the clearances to do exactly that — my first priority is keeping you safe. Now I want you to push your seat back all the way and place your foot on the dash to elevate your leg. Can you do that?" He stared at her so long that she waved a hand at him.

"Pay attention to the road. I don't want to drive off a cliff next!" She worked her jeans up her calf.

"Good, now take the blanket and press it hard to your wound to try to stop the bleeding."

"I'll ruin the blanket."

"Jesus Christ, Pip! Do it now."

With shaking hands, she did his bidding. He only drove a mile down the road before Josiah called, firing off questions. Ross's attention swung between his brother and the woman bleeding in the passenger seat.

Fucking hell. He'd failed her. By letting down his guard for a second, he'd placed her in harm's way.

She could have been killed. If she had, how would he ever explain that to her mother? Her father?

How would he live with himself?

"I want you, Boone and Silas with me in Seattle," he ordered Josiah as he stared blindly at the landscape. Any other time, driving through these mountains filled him with peace and gave his spirit a break from the mundane chores of the ranch or dealings with the company. Now he hardly noticed the rugged beauty that inspired awe.

"Booking the flights now. What else do you need? Should I call another agency for support? A solo protection officer in the area? How 'bout ex-military? I'm sure I can round up one or two. Or...maybe The Guard?"

He considered the question. The Guard was an elite group of retired military who operated mainly on the East Coast, but they were known to take on missions in Europe and as far as Russia.

"It's a good idea. Find out if any of them are in our area, and if so, plan my next stops and have them waiting there to back me up."

"I had a bad feeling about you taking this job, Ross." Josiah's ominous tone rang like a gong in Ross's soul.

"What do you mean?" His gritty tone drew Pippa's head around.

"I should have voiced it before you left. I should have insisted on coming with you."

"We needed you there. Working intel. None of us could have guessed this would happen."

"Is Pippa okay? She said she was hurt."

"A bullet grazed her calf."

"Jesus H Christ!"

"I'm getting her someplace where I can tend to her, but it's shallow. She's going to be okay." He met her stare when he said this.

She had to be okay.

But he wouldn't blame her one damn bit if she never trusted him again.

"Josiah."

"Yeah, bro?"

"No more fucking around and spinning wheels about hiring people. This is exactly what I've been talking about at the last five meetings we've had. We

105

need to scale up—and this incident shows us how much."

"I'll put the pressure on Noah and talk to Boone."

"Do that." He ended the call.

"What's the plan, Ross?" Pippa's voice wobbled.

He studied her for signs of shock. Her eyes were lucid and she was paler but not too bad. He touched the back of her hand, finding it warm.

"I'm not going into shock if that's what you're thinking," she said.

His lips quirked. "Forgot you're far smarter than me when it comes to bodies and what makes them tick. My plan's to get you the hell out of these mountains and then we're taking a detour instead of a straight shot to Seattle."

"I don't understand any of this. Nobody's ever shown me anything but kindness and excitement about my discovery."

"And I don't understand how much of the credit you get versus MIZR."

She brushed her hair off her face and bound it into a messy bun on the back of her head. "I work for MIZR but I receive credit for everything I discover. They only provide me with a lab and all I need. But what I find, they have the rights to use the technology."

"Meaning, you could sell the information to somebody else." He spoke slowly.

"Why would I do that? I'm loyal to MIZR."

"But not everyone feels the same, I'm sure."

"So you think...somebody's trying to steal my research and sell it to another lab? Or use it for himself?"

"It makes more sense than anything we've come up with so far." He gave her a sharp look and then reached behind the seat for water. He passed her a bottle and told her to drink.

"Stay hydrated, he says," she muttered, taking a sip.

Relieved by her sass, he said, "I need to ask about your personal life."

She lowered the bottle. "You listened to me pee, Ross. I think you're pretty well acquainted."

He grunted. "I mean I need names of anybody you've dated in your field, going back to university. Actually, I need names of all the people you've slept with, including one-night stands."

She lapsed into one of her silent spells. What in the hell could be going on in that brain of hers? She was probably alphabetizing her lovers.

Two pink spots burned on her cheeks.

"How many are there?" he finally burst out.

Those spots turned a flaming red. The tips of her ears too. "Three! What do you think I am?"

His pulse, hammering before, kicked into a gallop. Christ, he shouldn't care about her lovers, especially at a time like this. But what she said pleased him — a lot.

He passed her his phone. "Give Josiah the details."

She snatched the phone from him with enough strength to prove that she hadn't lost too much blood from the graze on her calf. She was in the middle of texting when the phone rang in her hand.

"It's Josiah," she said.

He took the device from her and brought the phone to his ear.

"Okay, The Guard's actually got two guys in our region. One on his way north from Vegas. He's our closest. He can be airlifted by private craft and meet you when you reach the Washington border."

He mentally mapped out his location and the length of time it would take to reach the border. He was pulling all the strings—favors too—but it was his best bet.

"Get him there. Find us a motel, something small and out of the way. I need to stop and tend to her wound better."

"Okay, this guy's name is Roman. A big, bad-ass motherfucker. I've met him."

"That's what I need. And Pippa's sending you a couple more names. Run them through the system."

After they ended the call, Pippa continued texting Josiah her information. Then Ross fished around behind the seat again and located the first-aid kit. "Open this," he said, dropping it in her lap. "Poor some antiseptic on your wound. We can't risk infection, and it'll be a while before we stop."

With a blank expression, she went about cleaning her gash, only wincing once.

"Good girl. Now wrap it in clean gauze."

He'd felt helpless before—plenty of times on the ranch where they lost an animal or when he'd stood at his grandfather's deathbed, knowing he couldn't do a damn thing to keep him alive. But not being able to help Pippa with this small task for fear of being jumped again if he stopped hit a whole new level.

Their eyes met.

And he glanced away.

* * * * *

Watching two big, tough guys exchange a chin nod of greeting would send any woman with eyes and a pair of ovaries into a tizzy.

Ross led her past the big, buff dude with arms that could shred a man, and entered the small off-the-beaten-path motel with only six rooms—all of them vacant besides the one she and Ross had been given.

At Ross's insistence, she leaned on him to take the weight off her leg. He closed the door, locked it, including the chain, dropped her bag and did a sweep of the room, checking in the bathroom and under the king-sized bed, and then walked back to her.

She stared at his hands. Images of his fists still curled after he stopped beating their attacker kept rising up in her mind.

She knew he was deadly, and now he'd proved it. He'd killed a man—for her. She should feel more sickened by the thought, and maybe she was in shock, but she could only believe the man attacking them knew what he was getting into when he took the job.

Who hired him?

"Sit down on the bed." Ross's order broke into her thoughts.

He helped her the two feet to the bed, and she sank to the stiff mattress covered in a striped bedspread.

"This place looks better on the inside than out," she remarked.

He knelt in front of her and unzipped the first-aid bag again. When locating the antiseptic and gauze, she'd seen a lot of things in that bag that made her question what the Wyntons and their colleagues got themselves into. Vials of antibiotics, morphine syrettes, medical staples, tweezers and clamps. A tourniquet.

She issued a sigh that came out shakier than she felt.

Ross's green eyes creased with worry. "I'm going to help you remove your jeans, honey."

A flutter hit her stomach.

"It's better to bandage your bare leg and then you can slide clean clothes on over it."

"Of course."

She'd already used the bathroom with him standing nearby. Getting naked in front of him was no big deal, right?

She hesitantly reached for her button and zipper. He busied himself removing items from the first-aid kit and laying them out on a big, sterile cloth, which he removed from a wrapper. She shifted to her feet in order to shimmy the denim over her hips.

Ross glanced up and then looked away.

She gave a nervous laugh. "Birthing hips."

"What?" He stared at her.

"A friend in college called my hips birthing hips one time we changed in front of each other."

He latched his gaze to her rounded hips, and the touch of his eyes scorched her. "Your friend's a dumb shit. Your hips are perfect."

She swallowed hard. He was only being a nice guy.

"You're too tall to ever really carry weight, Pippa." He shook his head and then removed his hat. When he set it next to her on the bed, she had a sudden urge to reach out and touch the white felt cloth which was an extension of Ross.

He helped her remove the jeans the rest of the way, careful when he reached the bullet graze on the back of her leg.

She inspected the wound along with him. "Have you ever been shot?"

His dark brows drew together. "No," he gritted out. "And I'm damn sorry you did."

Long seconds passed as he proceeded to examine the wound. Then he cleaned and bandaged it. When he withdrew one of the vials, he said, "You're not allergic to penicillin, are you?"

"No." She shucked the jacket she still wore and rolled up her sleeve, presenting her upper arm to him to inject. After the deed was done, they looked at each other.

"Good job. You didn't even flinch."

Now that she was safe for the moment and wasn't in danger of dying of sepsis from her wound, something else happened—her stomach clenched in gnawing hunger.

One thought of that juicy burger dropped back in the parking lot and the tears started to flow.

"Jesus, honey. Fuck." Still kneeling before her, he cupped her face. Brushed her hair off her forehead. "Are you in pain? I have something for that."

She shook her head with a loud sniffle. "I lost my burger."

"You..." He closed his eyes and opened them again. "At least it wasn't your life, honey."

Their stares met. The hunger inside her switched to a new kind—for Ross.

She threw herself at him.

His solid steel body felt warm, comforting, arousing...amazing.

Arms latched around his neck, she tipped her face for his kiss. A glimmer in his green eyes was his only hesitation before he claimed her lips.

Slamming his mouth over hers, he stood with her in his arms, settling on the bed with her legs draped over his lap as he intensified the kiss. He swept his tongue over the seam of her lips and plunged inside on her gasp.

Need battered her. She wiggled closer and stroked her tongue against his on the second pass. The low growl she raised in his chest set her on fire, and she angled her head to deepen the kiss.

He worked his fingers through her hair, loosening her bun. Each warm digit sent heat trickling over her scalp, down her neck to her breasts. Her nipples throbbed for his hands on them. His mouth on them.

He suddenly pulled back, his stare riveted on her. "Honey, this is wrong."

"Does it feel wrong?" She couldn't guess where this boldness sprang from. She certainly never guessed she'd talk to Ross Wynton this way a few days ago. Maybe just getting shot awakened her to the fact that life was short.

She brushed her lips back and forth over his. They appeared so hard yet felt so soft. So perfect. She could have low blood sugar because the blueberry bars wore off long ago, but she didn't think that was the case. She wanted Ross—she always had. As a teen, she didn't even know what she wanted from him—now she did.

Judging by the bulge of his cock, he no longer thought of her as that gawky little girl.

When she skated her mouth over his again, his growl erupted into a primal noise that had her body primed.

For him.

He twisted her in his arms and spread her on the bed. Bracing his weight overtop her, he gazed into her eyes. "This changes everything."

"I don't want to go back," she whispered.

"You're in pain. Not thinkin' straight."

She dug her fingers into his hair that always slightly curled on his nape. "Ross...you know that's not true."

He swallowed hard enough to make his Adam's apple work up and down.

Then he kissed her again with an urgency that rocked her to the core. Her insides trembled. Her pussy ached and her panties were soaked. She rubbed on the bulge in his jeans, shaking for more...more of Ross...more of everything.

Each stroke of his tongue over hers stole her mind. When he glided his hand over her hip, she recalled his drawled words... *They're perfect.*

She worked her hands across his broad shoulders, learning the power coiled within of them. Landing on his spine, she did the same, memorizing each contour of muscle until she could draw them out in her mind if she wanted to.

He tore from the kiss, staring at her mouth and panting hard. "I need to stop, but goddamn if I can."

"Don't," she murmured, searching his eyes. Her belly dipped at the expression he wore—a dark heat of desire she'd never seen on him or anyone else before.

Desire for her.

"This moment could ruin our friendship."

"Or start a new one," she argued.

"I want to do things to you that your past three lovers never even thought of."

Her insides melted. Juices flooded her panties.

"I want you to show me."

"Fuck, honey..." He dropped his head as if battling himself.

When he raised it again, she read the promise in his gaze, jolting her back to that moment he climbed into the back seat during the snowstorm and waited for her to join him.

He pulled her shirt off before she could think. When he kissed a blazing path down her throat to the crests of her breasts, she closed her eyes and sucked in the feel of the man guarding her with his life.

"Beautiful." He dotted a perfect line of kisses from the top of one breast to the other. Her skin pebbled at the warm caresses.

She worked his shirt up, gliding her palms over his skin that was velvet coating iron. He moved to help her remove the garment, and their gazes caught and held as he popped the clasp of her bra.

"There's no coming back from this, Pippa."

She shook her head. "I don't care. I want you."

As he exposed her breasts, he groaned. With one fingertip, he teased her straining nipple with the faintest of touches. So soft she wondered if she imagined it. But then he lowered his mouth to her bud and took it between his lips and she knew this was no dream.

A sharp need made her rub against him as he sucked her nipples into hard peaks. He drew on her, gently at first and increasing the pressure until she thought she'd die from want. When he moved to her other breast, circling her nipple with his tongue first and then drawing on it the way he had the first, her insides clenched.

"I've never been so...close to coming," she rasped.

He raised his head and slanted a look at her. While holding her stare, he settled his hand over her pussy. Her soaked panties were no barrier against his hot fingers as he stroked her lightly. So lightly. She shook and clutched at his shoulders.

"Kiss me," she begged.

A groan escaped him as he captured her mouth and strummed her clit with torturous precision. He knew just how to string her out, turn her inside out and drive her toward an end so big that it almost frightened her.

The pain in her leg vanished, replaced by white-hot passion. As his fingertip crested her swollen clit once more, she sucked in a gasp. Quivering on the precipice.

"Fuck, are you gonna come for me? I haven't gotten started, honey." He shoved to his knees, hooked his fingers in the sides of her panties and pulled them off, very gently when he reached her calf.

With a dark look, he spread her legs and covered her clit with his mouth. She stifled a scream, drowning in bliss. Or what she perceived to be bliss before he teased her clit with purposeful sweeps of his lips and tongue.

Writhing, she arched off the bed. He sucked on her nubbin. Then he slipped the point of his tongue through her folds and thrust it into her pussy. Juices soaked her—and him. She gripped his shoulders tighter with each pass of his tongue between clit and entrance.

Ross was everything she knew he'd be—and more. And if she wasn't already halfway to loving him by now, then him giving her the orgasm of her life made her tumble the rest of the way.

Chapter Seven

He drove his tongue into her clenching, contracting, fucking soaking wet walls, his brain locked on one thing--getting more of her. His cock stood at full erection, throbbing and about to burst.

A knock sounded somewhere in the distance. Pippa twisted her hands in his hair and...

More knocking.

He raised his head as a final shudder of release ripped through her body and she collapsed to the mattress.

Tap tap tap. More insistently.

His haze of lust fled in a blink as he realized someone was knocking at the motel door, and he sure as hell didn't think it was housekeeping delivering towels.

Pippa tensed. "The door," she whispered in a voice dripping with fear but throatier from her release.

Setting his palm on her stomach to calm her, he rose to his feet. "Cover up. I'm going to answer it."

Without bothering to put his shirt on, he unlocked the door and opened it a crack with the chain still in place. Roman stared back at him.

Tossing a look toward Pippa, he stepped outside to speak with him.

If the guy questioned why he was shirtless, he didn't ask. He was all business as he spoke.

"Word came in from your brother. I guess he tried to reach you, but you didn't answer."

"Pippa was shot. I was taking care of her," he said tightly.

Roman went on, "Those two guys who attacked you were ID'd by the police who picked them up. One was DOA and the other will live to pay for his crimes. Both are common hired thugs."

"Fuck. That solidifies my suspicion that somebody knows where Pippa's headed. I don't believe we were followed, though. I think they hit gold when they found us at that rest stop."

Roman nodded. "I'd say you're right. They know you're headed to Seattle for the conference."

"They're hired to take me out and kidnap Pippa."

"Any chance of you *not* taking her to Seattle?"

Ross expelled a breath. "I don't know. But I'll try to convince her not to attend that conference. The thing they're after is the topic she's speaking about, unless I'm totally wrong."

Pines swayed in the wind sweeping through the hollow where the motel was located. Ross stared at them for a beat, considering a new tactic. "We can go to Seattle, lead them into a trap and tie the noose."

Roman lifted a fist, knuckles out. "That's the best plan I've heard today. I got your six, man."

Ross bumped knuckles with him. "We're only staying long enough for her to rest and clean up."

"I'll follow when you're ready."

They began to part ways, when Roman swung back. "Ya know, I've seen this a couple other times."

Ross narrowed his eyes. "Seen what?"

"A bodyguard falling for his ward. Pretty rampant in The Guard." He sliced a grin at Ross.

He'd heard a rumor or two.

Shaking his head at his words, Ross turned back to the door, preparing himself for what he had to do.

What he should have done long before he let Pippa get to him.

Quietly, he closed the door and secured the locks. She sat up, covers clutched against her nudity and her hair tumbling down. Her eyes so bright from the aftershocks of her release.

He swiped his tongue over his bottom lip, tasting her.

"What's happening?" she asked.

"We're going to get cleaned up and on the road again. But we're taking another route in hopes of losing anyone else who might be after you."

Disappointment hit her eyes, and she dropped her stare to her lap. Then she climbed off the bed, dragging the quilt with her. She paused to grab her bag he'd brought in. When she bent, the quilt edges parted, giving him a glimpse of a long, bare, honeyed thigh.

She'd be sticky wet between them. Fuck, the drive to bury his cock in her and keep her in bed for a week flared across his senses.

He shouldn't have gone this far with her. He'd never look at her again without tasting her...feeling her tense for him...feeling her pulse for him.

She closed the bathroom door and he issued a groan. He clenched his fists against the urge to whip open that door and pick up where they left off.

But he couldn't.

He grabbed his shirt and pulled it on. Then he swiped his fingers through his disheveled hair and located his phone. After he found the closest restaurant for takeout and ordered two burgers and fries for pickup in half an hour, he texted Boone.

Shit's going sideways.

I heard. Need me to drop the governor and come help sooner?

For a moment, he considered Boone leaving his post earlier than planned.

No, see it through and come to Seattle as planned.

Is Pippa okay? Josiah filled me in on what happened.

121

The bathroom door was closed. Ross heard nothing. If she was in there crying, he'd feel worse than ever.

Compressing his lips, he texted a reply. *She's fine.*

Wait — what? She tastes fine?

He blinked at the screen. Had he just texted what was in his mind?

Christ on a piece of toast, he had.

I mean she IS fine. Autocorrect.

Uh-huh.

Dick. Get back to your post.

Boone sent some laughing emojis.

Ross tossed his phone onto the bed and rammed his hat down. Then he adjusted his still swollen cock. He could end his torment by busting down that door, grabbing Pippa and pinning her to the wall.

He replayed that scenario in his mind several times. Things could go two ways — she responded with all the fervor she had minutes before. Or she could pull out her aikido and chop him in the balls. He deserved no less.

He texted Roman, letting him know where they'd stop for food and when, though he could just open the door and speak to him. After his reply, Ross flipped through emails. He was just reading the details about one of Pippa's exes and shaking his head at all the letters of his degrees following his name, when the bathroom door opened.

She stepped out, limping only slightly.

Avoiding his stare, she dropped the bag and put on her boots. Her hair was damp but not wet, drawn off her face in a ponytail. Her glasses slipped down her nose as she bent to zip her ankle boots.

An awkward silence hung between them, gathering by the second like storm clouds on the horizon of their relationship. To think they'd only experienced a ray of sun before he ruined it.

Why had he stopped?

When she straightened, he stared at her hips. Birthing hips his ass. They were just right. And the treasure between them was sweet honey.

He mentally linked her with the photo of the man in his email. Had that guy gotten a taste of Pippa? He had a cocky look most graduates of Ivy League schools did, which gave Ross the impression his own pleasure would come before his lover's.

"Your leg okay?" he asked.

"Yeah," she said breezily, picking up her computer bag and looping the strap across her body. The leather cut in between her breasts, outlining them against the simple black button-up shirt she wore.

He lowered his gaze to the rest of her, clad in slim-fitting black jeans that made her legs look a hundred miles long. While Corrine had chosen her clothes, she nailed it perfectly. Pippa had no need for flashy clothes or makeup or teased hair to be the most stunning woman in the room.

"I'm ready." She interrupted his thoughts.

123

"I need a minute." If he didn't wash her off his fingers and lips, he'd only make it five steps—to grab her and take her to bed.

Minutes later with Roman tailing them in a rental vehicle, Ross grabbed their food from the restaurant. When he dropped the bag into Pippa's lap, her face lit up. His heart thumped at the sight of her happy expression, and he couldn't look away while she unwrapped the burger and took the first bite.

He always preached to his employees that the ward required more than just a bodyguard. Sometimes, they needed soothing. To be made to feel human during the scariest times of their lives.

I gave her a burger, large fries and an orgasm. He'd say he fulfilled his duty. Too bad he hadn't taken a moment in the bathroom to pound his cock through his fist and ease his own throbbing balls.

"Here."

He pulled his attention from the road to the burger Pippa had partially unwrapped and held out to him.

Her shoulders still set with a tenseness that wasn't there before he crossed boundaries, but at least she wasn't giving him the silent treatment.

"Thanks for the burger," she said farther down the road.

"No thanks needed, Pip."

Her chest heaved once, and then she pulled the blanket over herself.

124

Miles passed. They hit a patch of freezing drizzle, which he commented on but she refused to respond to him.

His chest burned, and a heavy concrete weight settled there.

Until she began to ignore him, he didn't realize how much he wanted to hear her voice.

* * * * *

"Josiah, I need you to run an Idaho plate. Mike Kilo Papa niner seven two."

Pippa roused from her deep thoughts about Ross and shifted in her seat to look at their surroundings. They'd been on the road for hours, and this road trip was longer and more stressful than sharing a back seat in her parents' Subaru with her annoying little sister.

She spotted the vehicle with the license plate Ross recited to Josiah. The plain white SUV wasn't giving her any bad vibes, but then again, she wasn't trained to scope out danger.

"Do you think that SUV is suspicious?" Her voice sounded clearer after resting it some. Her throaty moans back in the motel probably hadn't helped it.

"Dunno, but we've been playing road tag for about ten miles now."

The SUV dropped speed, which meant they caught up to it. But Ross let off the gas to stay a few car lengths behind.

She glanced in the side mirror to see Roman following them in a black SUV. They'd driven out of the freezing drizzle, but snow stuck to the road and drifted in the open places.

"Leave it to me to choose the worst time for travel," she said.

"We'll leave the snow and ice behind once we hit the coast."

Seattle. Her family. A warmth washed over her at the thought of being with them all again. Right now, she could really use a hug from her parents and sister.

"Do you think I'll have time to spend with my family?" she asked.

Ross kept his attention centered on that white SUV with the Idaho plate. "I'd like to say yes, but fact is, I don't know, Pippa. It's hard to say what we'll get into with the conference. And your family will be locked down and guarded."

She gasped. "You're kidding!"

The grim set of his lips told her he wasn't remotely playing with her.

"Oh God. They're going to be so worried."

"Boone, Josiah and Silas will be there, along with Roman. Hopefully we can settle their fears."

"Holly's coming in from Portland just to spend the weekend with me. She rarely gets leave from her job, and I hate to spoil her vacation."

"It's not your fault, Pippa."

"Did your team find anything on the threatening note?"

"The handwriting doesn't come up in the database, which means the person who wrote it has never been arrested." He pierced her in his stare. "Pippa, about what happened at the motel —"

She felt like plugging her ears with her fingers and singing over whatever he had to say. "We don't need to discuss it."

It was only the best orgasm of my life with the only man I can imagine giving myself to at this point.

"Yes, we damn well do need to discuss it."

"I'm good."

"Don't be stubborn."

"Stubborn? You're the one who *stubbornly* held himself back. I bet you're still aching, since you didn't get off. Am I right?"

He swerved over the line. A car honked at him, and he quickly righted the truck. "Yes, I'm aching. You have no idea."

"Good."

"Good?" he shot back.

Exhilaration hit her veins, thickening them with desire too. Why did this argument feel like foreplay?

"You got what you wanted — which was nothing."

He groaned and centered his palm over his groin, nudging his swelling cock to give it more room. "You drive me crazy, Pip."

"Not crazy enough for you to finish the job."

"Because I'm focusing on this job!" He waved a hand at the SUV, which probably belonged to some harmless traveler oblivious to Ross's suspicions. "You asked me to keep you safe. Not take you to bed!"

"Pretty sure I asked for that too." Why was she pushing him? Goading him? Maybe to break down that hard wall she never could demolish before.

A low noise similar to a growling wolf came from the driver's seat. "It isn't as if I don't want to, Pippa. But I have to stay focused. You were already injured on my watch. Things could have been much worse. I couldn't live with myself if something happened to you."

He ended on a fainter, grittier note than she'd ever heard from him before. It touched her.

Deep.

But he was right—neither of them could afford to let down their guards.

She nudged her glasses up and massaged her eyes. "You're right."

He swung his head from the road to look at her. "You're agreeing with me?"

"Why do you sound ticked off about that? I thought you'd want me to agree with you!"

"Ticked off," he muttered.

"Pissed off," she amended in Ross Wynton style.

He zeroed in on her lips. "I shouldn't say this, but I love it when you cuss."

Her insides clenched with fresh heat never quite satisfied from before. It took her a moment to catch her breath. "Really?"

"Yes. Dammit. Really." He glared at the backs of vehicles spread out over the few miles they could see on the flat stretch.

How did she even process that claim from the cowboy? "Why?" she finally asked.

He worked his jaw, and the dimple flashed though he wasn't smiling. "It's knowing you— knowing you before. When you were just a goodie two-shoes kid."

"So the good girl turned bad appeals to you?"

"Somethin' like that. And it's the glasses too."

She sat against the seat in surprise. "The glasses?"

"Stop asking me these questions, Pippa. You know what you do to me."

That rang with finality, but she had no idea what she did to him any more than before he went down between her thighs and licked her to a blazing orgasm.

Her insides were hot and sticky with need, and one look at Ross's lap revealed he suffered the same way. That gave her a bit of satisfaction, at least.

They continued to drive.

She started to feel claustrophobic from sitting in the truck so long. The tension hovering between her and Ross wasn't helping matters. She must be losing her mind. Acting neurotic. Erratic. She only wanted to get to Seattle, see her family and speak at the conference.

The late afternoon sun sat at an angle that made her wish she could don a pair of sunglasses. Instead, she flipped the visor down to provide some shade.

Her phone buzzed.

Ross looked at her. "You know the drill."

"It's Meredith."

"Pippa," he said with an edge of warning.

She rolled her eyes and answered the call on speakerphone.

"Pippa, thank goodness I reached you. I called your house like a dozen times."

"Aww, thanks, Meredith. That was really sweet of you, but I was asleep most of the day."

"Then I swung by your apartment and buzzed you until the doorman told me you weren't in."

Sending a sideways glance at Ross, Pippa said, "Yes, I'm out. I just went to urgent care."

"Oh no! So you're really ill?"

"Just the flu. Bad luck." She hoped her lies came off as real, but Ross didn't indicate otherwise.

"You sound like you're in the car."

"I am. They prescribed me that flu medicine, and I'm on my way to the pharmacy to pick it up."

"I'm so sorry to hear you're sick. Remember when one of us would be sick in college and we'd bring each other care baskets stuffed with medicine and cough drops and cans of soup?"

She smiled. "And Oreos."

Ross's lips twitched at the corner.

"I can bring you a care basket later, Pippa," Meredith said.

Panic swept over her. "That's really sweet of you, but I'd hate to give you the virus too. I'm fine really."

"Will you still be able to fly to Seattle? The altitudes will be hell on your sinuses."

"Yes, I'll be fine. I won't miss the conference."

"Well, that's a relief to everyone attending. You *are* the diamond of the whole scientific world right now."

Ross's knuckles grew white on the wheel.

"Thanks for always trying to cheer me up, Meredith. I'm almost to the pharmacy now. I'll talk to you soon."

"Take care, my friend."

She ended the call, and two heartbeats passed before Ross spoke.

"The diamond of the scientific world," he repeated.

"It's nothing. She's just boosting me to make me feel better."

"But people really do think of you that way because of your finding."

She met his gaze. Before he kissed her and sucked her nipples—then her clit—she believed she knew how deep his eyes really were. Now she saw so much more. They resembled two green forests. The trees at the front appeared lighter, but the closer she looked, the more she saw the darker shadowed areas deep within.

A quiver began in her lower belly and slipped down between her legs.

"I guess they do think of me as important. Until next year when someone else makes a discovery."

"I don't think they're going to top you, Pippa. And that means one thing to me—that even after this, you're still in the spotlight. You're not out of danger."

A shudder rippled down her spine, icy fingers digging in and spreading over her skin. "Well, you can't be my bodyguard forever," she said with a light laugh to cover her nerves.

Ross fisted a hand and brought it to his mouth as if to trap any words from escaping.

Chapter Eight

Saying Pippa was different from the girl he'd known would be like saying the sky was down and the earth up.

She set him off-balance.

She drove him crazy.

And he fucking loved every minute of it.

Part of his reason for wanting to hear her cuss resulted directly from him loving how she'd grown in the past decade. Hearing her say the F word or beg for his mouth on her reminded him that she was *not* the kid who hung out with him and his brothers on the ranch.

Yet she was still off-limits. To hurt her would invite the wrath of not only her father but his own, along with every Wynton in Stone Pass. Hell, even his buddy Silas would give him hell for breaking Pippa's heart.

All he could offer her was a one-night stand, like all the other ladies he'd been with. He was at the prime of his career. He couldn't take time for relationships, family and all the crap that came with it. He'd seen enough of what his little brother, Noah, went through with his ex-girlfriend, before he found the love of his life Maya Ray.

Ross couldn't only pump the brakes when it came to stopping his crazy libido where Pippa was concerned — he slammed them.

The second time he passed a sign for a canyon, he pulled out his phone and dialed Roman.

"What's happening?" Roman asked.

"I'm going to make a stop."

Pippa pushed her glasses up her nose as she often did when thoughtful.

"Next exit? At the canyon?" Roman asked.

"Yes."

"Your gas tank low? I thought you filled up."

"I need a break. I've been driving for hours."

"I'm right behind you," Roman said.

When Ross ended the call, Pippa spoke up, "I can drive for a bit."

"You're injured."

"You said yourself it's only a graze. I've had deeper cuts from shaving."

His real reason for wanting to stop wasn't because he'd spent long hours behind the wheel — he really wanted to spend a few minutes of solitude with her. Take in the beautiful scenery and maybe make a memory.

His thinking was a complete one-eighty from minutes before when he made the decision to back away. Yeah, his judgment might be more than a little clouded by all her cute little mannerisms like pushing her glasses up or chewing at the same fingernail. Not to mention the breathy cries of pleasure echoing through his mind.

The road to the canyon pitched steeply, but then leveled off in a place where they could park. When he got out, Roman did too. Ross nodded to him as he checked the gun at his waistband, ensuring he had a good grip if he needed it.

When Ross opened the passenger door, Pippa twisted to face him. "Am I allowed to get out and walk around?"

Christ, her beauty stole his breath. Those plump lips had a natural pink flush that made him want to kiss her harder—to use her mouth—just to see them turn red.

Their gazes clung. Finally, he held out a hand to her. She slipped hers into it, and he assisted her to the ground.

She winced at the first step, and he stopped. "You don't have to do this."

"I need to move. My butt's falling asleep."

One look at her backside told him that *he* was very much alive and kicking, at least. The rounded globes begged for him to cup them and lift her against his erection. Fuck, what had he been thinking to stop and sightsee?

He slowly led her across a rocky path leading to a lookout over a canyon. The white sky against the gray rock and dark pines stole his breath—or so he thought before his gaze landed on Pippa.

His heart caught. Hell, it beat out of time.

She twisted to meet his stare, and what she saw on his face made her lips part.

"I'm sorry in advance."

She blinked. "For what?"

"This." He hooked a hand around her nape and drew her mouth to his. Dark passion loomed beneath the surface, and it burst out the moment he tasted her.

A soft moan escaped her lips, snatched by the wind, but he took the next one and fed it back to her with a groan of his own. With a hand on the small of her back, he drew her against him. As she twisted the cloth of his coat, his heart gave another hard jerk.

"Ross," she murmured between sweeping passes of his tongue.

"Pippa..." His own tone came out like gravel under his boot.

"Don't ever apologize for this." She leaned into him.

He pulled away with no intention of going back for more—but he did. What about her drove him to the brink of insanity? His brothers would believe he jumped into the gorge before they'd buy a story about him stopping to woo her in a beautiful place.

Cupping her face, he applied pressure to her chin, causing her to open wider for his tongue. When he plunged inside, there wasn't any turning back from this now. He'd torn down too many fences, and now the bull was in the pasture, so to speak.

Ross would have her, if only for one night of madness.

When he withdrew, he slowly peeled his fingers off her one at a time, each fingertip reluctant to leave her body. He took a step back.

Her hazel eyes glimmered with the heat he'd only given her a few short minutes to experience.

"I wish I could take a selfie of us here. It's beautiful," he rasped.

"You're not looking at the scenery."

"I have better things to look at than a bunch of rock walls."

Her soft smile and the way she tucked her chin swelled his heart.

Taking her hand, he led her back to the truck. Roman leaned against his SUV. Seeing them, he straightened and circled to the driver's door. If he had questions about what they were doing—or had seen them—he didn't say.

Ross broke the code of honor a bodyguard lived by. If one of his employees at WEST Protection laid a hand on his ward, Ross would fire him, brother, cousin, friend or otherwise. Rationalizing that he and Pippa would be equally as attracted to each other if she'd come to the ranch for a friendly visit wouldn't make it right, even if it was absolutely true.

As he assisted her into the truck, he saw her wince. "You're taking painkillers."

"Fine, but I only need a couple pills, not the morphine in your first-aid kit."

He quirked a smile at her and retrieved the kit from the back seat. After he handed her a bottle of water and dropped two pills into her cupped palm, he couldn't resist reaching out and brushing his thumb across her lips.

"They're swollen," he murmured. "I'd say I'll be gentler next time I kiss you, but I'd be lyin'."

Her breasts heaved as she sucked in a sharp breath at his words.

Driving back to the exit to get on the highway lulled him into a sense that everything would be okay. He'd get Pippa safe. Even the weather was cooperating, the deep gray snow clouds breaking up to create an expanse of white sky.

As they entered the roadway, he checked his side mirror—and spotted a vehicle flying up next to him. He braked but not before they were cut off.

Pippa gasped and braced a hand on the dash.

He saw the driver of the other vehicle raise his arm. In a blink, Ross assessed the danger.

"Get down!" he barked to Pippa.

She folded in half as a volley of bullets sprayed his truck. He whipped out his weapon to defend them. Roman hit the gas and zoomed by in pursuit. Ross's phone buzzed.

"Where the hell did they come from?" Roman demanded.

"No fucking clue. I'm hanging back. I can't put my ward in the line of fire." No sooner did the words leave his mouth that he glanced in his rearview to see another vehicle bearing down on him. Roman took off after the shooters in a high-speed chase, which left Ross on his own.

"What's going on?" Pippa cried.

"Don't lift your head. Stay. Down." He stomped the gas to outrun the asshole coming at them from behind. All his tactical training kicked in. He gauged distance, speed and calculated the velocity of his bullet.

"Ross!"

"I'm handling it. Just do as I say," he commanded her.

Up ahead Roman and the other car were engaged in a rolling shootout, and if Ross didn't get the hell away from this other pursuer, he'd be in the same situation with Pippa.

"Hold on." He hit a speed of eighty. Then eighty-five. The vehicle kept up. Why had he agreed to take this highway? On a back road, he'd have side roads to jump on and lose this motherfucker.

Pippa's labored breathing reached into his brain and snapped his focus to her.

"Take slow breaths. You're hyperventilating."

"Wynton, what's your status?" Roman's voice came at him.

"Holding my own. Can't shake this guy off my tail."

"Try to cut across the median and into the eastbound lane."

"Never make it through that deep snow. I'm going to take a shot," Ross said.

Pippa issued a strangled cry.

If he could hit a tire, he'd make a getaway.

He also ran the risk of being shot in return.

"I'll get you first, you bastard. Come on." He let off the gas, dropping back to allow the pursuer to catch up. As soon as he had the car within firing range, he hit the brakes. The truck went into a skid, the back end fishtailing to the right as they started into a donut.

"Oh God!" Pippa screamed.

Ross had a perfect shot. He'd never fired through a windshield before, but he'd seen it demonstrated. His stare jumped between the rear tire of the vehicle to the figure in the driver's seat.

The truck continued in its skid, but he had control. As they swung past the vehicle, he fired.

* * * * *

Pippa had never hyperventilated in her entire life. Not when she was on that swinging bridge over a precipice during her time in Asia and she realized just how deep her fear of heights ran. Not even after her attack in the airport, though she'd been dizzy from breathing so hard.

The truck seemed to spin. Then she realized it really was spinning on the roadway. If being out of control wasn't scary enough, the shots Ross fired made her blood run cold in her veins. She lifted her head to see him firing straight through the windshield.

"Get down!"

She dropped her face to her knees again, fear an icy cloak. She started to shiver.

More popping sounds had her heart stalling in her chest.

"They're shooting at us!" she cried out.

Ross said nothing — he was engaged in a battle for their lives. He brought the truck out of the donut with all the ease of a stunt driver. Which way was which? Without her vision, for all she knew, they were facing backward on the road.

"Holy shit!" he burst.

"What's happening?"

"Stay down! Roman drove that other vehicle off the road and it just flipped about eight times."

"Is Roman okay?"

The man's voice projected through Ross's speakers. "I'm fine. Even the jaws of life can't help that bastard, though."

"I have to get us out of this situation." Ross's voice was tight.

Next thing she knew the vehicle surged forward, picking up speed by the second. Terror had Pippa clinging to the seat, her fingers aching from holding on so tight.

She wished she could see what was happening. Anticipating them flipping eight times like that other vehicle, or Ross being shot, tore her apart with terror.

A whir of a window going down stood the hair up on her nape. Freezing air rushed over her.

Ross fired five shots in a row. "Yes!"

She couldn't resist jerking upright, danger or not. She swept her gaze over the roadway to see they were facing forward, and the other vehicle zigzagged all over the place before leaving the road.

The vehicle hit the snow humped on the side from the snowplow and launched upward. Flipped. And continued to roll.

"Hell yeah!" Roman exclaimed as he spotted the victory.

She threw a look at Ross. His jaw clenched into a steel vise, but he didn't speak or look her direction.

"I have to get us the fuck off this road. Roman, get us on a better route."

"Got it. Follow me."

As Ross drove by the wreckage, she turned to try to make out any survivor.

"Did you...shoot the driver?" Her voice wobbled.

"Yes." How he slipped the syllable out between his tight jaw, she had no clue.

"How did they find us? What is happening?"

"Pippa, give me your phone."

Her eyes widened. Her phone?

She scrabbled in her bag and held it up. "Why?"

"Hand it to me."

"It's my personal device. I don't think anyone—"

The blazing fury in his eyes stopped her.

Gulping, she held out the phone. Was it possible someone was tracking her through it?

He dropped it to the floor by his feet, jerked his knee upward and then crushed her phone under his boot. Several stomps later, he reached down and lifted the busted remains. He opened the window and hurled it out.

The cold air worked another shiver through her, but so did the truth of the situation.

More lives than her own were on the line. She'd put Ross, and Roman too, in danger. In her crunched pose, she had no idea what the roadway must have looked like, but she pictured them using their vehicles like steel horses. In their younger years, Ross and his

143

brothers used to race, and she could still see them galloping fast and furious across the fields.

"Do you think they were tracking me through my phone?"

"Most likely." He glanced toward her feet, where her computer bag sat.

Panic rushed through her. "No way. It can't be my computer too—it's secured with top level passwords and my thumbprint. Nobody could enter it. Not even MIZR."

"I wouldn't be so sure about that," he muttered. "You might believe your company and everyone in it is on your side, but at least one person is your enemy, Pippa. Wake up and look at what's going on."

She held the breath until her lungs burned.

He was right.

Someone she worked with, maybe even closely in the lab, backed these attacks. They wanted her data enough to threaten her life, along with those of her bodyguards. They hunted her to the airport in Detroit and now to the West Coast.

"M-maybe I shouldn't go to Seattle," she whispered.

He swung his head toward her. "No, we're going. And as many of my men as I can muster will be there to lay a trap. We're going to put an end to this forever, Pippa." He twitched his jaw toward her laptop bag again. "If you won't let me smash the fucking thing, then you're going to let my men analyze it."

Seeing no other way around his demand, she nodded.

The quivery feelings he'd raised in her with his kisses on the edge of that canyon hardened into dark coals. Ross Wynton's kisses made her forget her reason for being with him. It lured her into a false sense of security, and for those few breathless, heart-pounding seconds, she stopped being afraid.

They'd been driving for what felt like days now. Everything started to look the same. Mountains in the distance, snow and sky.

After an hour of silence, Ross said, "I'm sorry I had to break your phone."

"I understand."

"Usually the first thing a person ditches when they're on the run is their phone."

"Since I've never been on the run, I never thought of it."

"Of course not, honey."

The endearment trickled through her, bathing her with warmth.

"We're stopping for the night so you can sleep."

She studied his profile. Lines rimmed his eyes, from stress, fatigue or both. She'd caused those lines.

Minutes later they turned into a sleepy little town. She'd believe it to be abandoned if not for a random vehicle parked in front of the bar or small grocery store. The motel was as small as the last, clad in dark wood siding and the tan shutters lent a quaint appeal. A carved bear stood sentry next to the hand-hewn sign declaring a vacancy.

"Where are we?" she asked.

"Somewhere in Washington." Ross's humor gave her the first glimpse of his old self since the shootout.

"That's good enough."

Roman went inside to secure two rooms. She hated how her heart beat too fast and her legs felt weak when she left the safety of the truck to follow him to the room. With two big men sandwiching her the entire walk from parking lot to motel, she felt much more important than she actually was.

While Ross searched the room, she sank to the bed and pulled her jeans up to inspect the wound on her calf.

Ross walked out of the bathroom after inspecting every corner. His gaze landed on her. "Are you in pain?"

"It stings a little but it's fine."

"Is it hot?"

"I know how to look for infection. Besides, that penicillin shot should kill off anything. Where did you get your first-aid kit? A farm supply store?"

His lips twitched. "We have our sources."

They faced each other.

His eyes burned with anger unlike anything she'd ever seen before.

Shocked silent, she peeled off her coat and dropped it to the nearby chair.

He did the same, and his eyes never lost that flicker of fury.

She stared past him at a photo on the wall of two bear cubs playing in a river. Well, maybe she was mad too. At the situation. With the person pursuing her. And the fact several people had died now as a result.

She also wanted to slip into bed and find some escape.

Grabbing the hem of her top, she ripped it overhead and kicked off her boots.

Ross watched her a moment and then did the same until he stood shirtless and in socked feet in front of her.

When she reached to the button of her jeans, his hands dropped too.

"How long are we staying?" To hell with sleep— she found a new escape plan.

She slid down her zipper.

He was a step behind her, working open his belt. "Only long enough to catch a few hours of sleep."

Staring straight at him, she shoved her jeans down her hips and stepped out of them. He traced her every move, his gaze locking her in place. Tingles zipped along her nerves, and her nipples hardened at the brush of his eyes over her skin.

He set his handgun on the small fake wood table and shed his jeans too.

Her breath caught. Facing the nearly naked man in her bra and panties unnerved the hell out of her.

"Why are you angry with me?" she spat.

His eyes appeared to darken. In one step he reached her. He wrapped his arms around her and lifted her against him. Staring into her eyes, he rumbled, "I'm not angry with you. I'm furious with the people after you."

Then he crushed his mouth to hers.

They fell to the bed. Grabbing her thigh, he pulled her leg up around his hip. His erection rubbed against her neediest point. As he ground his cock into her, she parted her lips on a cry.

He captured her mouth again, plunging his tongue inside to stroke across hers. Dark hunger gripped her. She was under the Ross Wynton spell. As a teen, it hadn't occurred to her they could be like this...but some innate sense told her if he ever touched her, it would be primal and urgent.

It was better than her girlish fantasies.

Pattering her fingers over the muscles layered on his spine, she gripped his shoulders. With a groan, he rocked his cock into her again. And again.

"You better not stop halfway through like last time," she warned.

He wore the same intense, dead serious expression. "Not a chance."

He attacked her throat, setting her on fire with blazing kisses and the coarse stubble of his angled jaw. She squeezed her eyes shut, losing herself in the only man she could see herself wanting for the rest of her days.

He bit into her earlobe, and her pussy squeezed as though he knew the location of her button and when to press it. While she explored his body with her hands, she rubbed against him. The swollen head of his cock nudged her clit. His sharp groan rocked her.

Twisting her head, she found his mouth. They collided with a bruising crush of lips. Her core pulsed. Her panties were drenched.

Ross skated a hand over her breast, barely brushing her aching nipple — where had her bra gone? — and continued on. When he hooked his finger in her panties and pulled the soaking cloth aside, her heart trilled.

Gazing into her eyes, he rubbed his cock over her bared slit.

She shoved his underwear over his buttocks. "Take these off," she rasped.

He pushed off the bed, biceps flexing by her ears, and stood at the end of the bed. Chest heaving, he slowly drew her panties down her hips and off her feet.

She stopped breathing. A glance from the man left her panting. If he didn't touch her soon, she'd...she'd...combust.

Planting a knee on the mattress, he leaned over her. Watching her reaction, he worked his fingertips up her inner thigh and paused at her center.

Lines of tension formed around his hard lips.

"Don't stop," she rasped.

In one thrust, he stretched her with two fingers. Maybe it was three—she couldn't think beyond the extreme pleasure of him fingering her.

Or his intense stare as he watched what he did to her. She thrashed against his fingers, taking him deeper inside her until she had no idea of anything separating them from being one person.

Totally lost and not caring what happened to her after this, she gave herself up to his slow, thorough plunges and frantic, come-for-me thrusts. Her breaths came out as sobs and her heart tripled its beat. The scientist in her took note of her body reacting to his nearness—a rise in hormones. A dump of endorphins in her brain.

He dragged his tongue over his lower lip. "Don't try to hold back with me, honey. I always get what I want."

Chapter Nine

She was holding back, goddammit, and he wouldn't have it. He didn't want some half-cocked orgasm from the woman. He wanted wild abandon. Primal screams. He wanted her to soak his fingers and the bed beneath her.

As he worked his digits in and out of her tight canal, he monitored her face. When he glided his fingertip over one spot, her eyelids fluttered. Her pulse flickered faster at the base of her throat.

He withdrew his fingers and swirled them over her clit, forcing it into a stiff bud. She thumped her heel on the mattress in dismay.

"You want more of this?" He dipped only the tips of his fingers into her pussy.

She cried out.

"Or this?" He pulled free and stuck out his long tongue.

"Oh God!"

He knelt at the side of the bed. Her pussy was inches from his lips and tongue, and the scent of her arousal had his cock pounding. His blood pounding.

151

He spread her thighs and flattened his tongue over her clit. She arched on a cry.

Using all he'd ever learned about pleasuring a woman, he doubled his efforts on Pippa. Whatever force drove him to give her the best experience of her life had him eating her pussy like a fucking wild man.

He flicked her core with the tip of his tongue. He sucked her until her hips rose off the bed. When that wasn't enough for him, he clasped both nipples, teasing, tormenting and twisting them.

Her legs shook. She threw her legs over his shoulders and bucked into his mouth as her cries mingled with his grunts of absolute need.

Releasing his suction on her clit, he moved down her slick folds to tongue her entrance. Then he teased a finger through her buttocks to nestle against her pucker.

"Ross!" Her throaty rasp stole his last shred of control.

He coated his finger in her wetness and eased inside her tight sheath to the first knuckle.

Her chest heaved.

"Easy, honey. Let me inside. I promise you'll like it."

He lapped at her clit again until her muscles unclenched and he slowly slid his finger in her backside all the way.

"Oh. My. God." She tensed, gave one huge quiver and began to come from the invasion coupled with his tongue strumming over her clit.

She came—and screamed his name. Over and over. If the walls were paper-thin as he suspected, Roman would hear every noise she made for him, and fuck if he gave a damn. He withdrew his finger and eased it back in as she came apart in shaking gasps.

Her hair fell over her eye, and her lips hung open on a final silent gasp.

Fuck, seeing her this way—so undone—flooded his chest with some need to claim all parts of her, body and soul.

"Ross?" The confusion in her tone made him look at her harder.

Then she wiggled her hips. Her inner muscles clenched on his finger, and he barely registered that she was about to come until she tremored, dragging his finger back inside her ass as a louder scream ripped from her throat.

In awe, he watched her come apart for him. The way she'd kissed him back on the ledge of that canyon told him she could be this way.

Now he knew.

Fuck if he ever wanted to stop pleasuring her.

He fucked his finger slowly in and out, laying his jaw on her thigh to watch her beautiful face flutter with pleasure and shock at what was happening to her.

When a last shudder tore through her body, their gazes met. The flush on her cheeks and the sparkle of sweat on her skin left him throbbing.

Gently, he brushed his jaw over her thigh. The rasping noise made her cry out again, and when he lifted his head, he left a pink mark.

"Ross...what was that? What did you do to me?"

With slow gentleness, he withdrew his finger from her backside. "I took what I wanted from you. And you're so...fucking...responsive."

It took an extreme act of will to walk away from her and use the bathroom. After washing his hands and splashing his face to cool off a margin before he claimed her fully, he dropped his boxers and walked out with his cock stiff and swaying with every step he took to the bed.

She sat up, breasts full and nipples erect. Her hair a mess and her bottom lip bitten.

He glanced between her thighs at her wet pussy, her clit barely peeking from between the folds, and his cock surged.

Scooting to the edge of the bed, she reached for him.

He let her clamp onto his ass and go so far as to draw the tip of his cock to her pretty lips.

"Fuck. I can't let you suck me into your hot mouth."

Her eyes glowed with desire. "I want to, Ross. Let me." She lowered her lips and brushed a kiss over the crest. Then she stuck out her tongue and stroked the slit, gathering his precum.

His eyes closed, and he locked his hands into fists at his sides to keep from grabbing her and burying his dick in her. Fucking her hard and rough and in all the ways a woman like her didn't deserve.

Unclenching his hands, he opened his eyes and stared down at her. "Not this time." He swung his hips, regretfully pulling his cock from her mouth.

He grabbed a condom from his wallet—his only fucking condom, dammit—and rolled it on. She watched with her nipples growing darker and heavier by the moment. When he stepped up to her again, he couldn't restrain himself.

He grabbed her, wrapped her legs around his hips and buried himself deep in a single thrust.

She went so still, his pulse pounded with fear that he'd hurt her. But then she bit into his shoulder.

A growl escaped him, and he churned his hips in an automatic reflex to move inside this tight, hot, sweet woman who'd been driving him crazy since he picked her up at the airport. Hell, if he analyzed it— and he analyzed everything—he'd say her call for help had been his true undoing.

The moment she took him by the heart and tugged.

He found her lips, waiting and eager. Their kiss raged on and on as he fucked her with slow gliding strokes. Deep—deeper. He thought of his finger buried in her ass and how she'd come for him that way, and he damn near lost it. His balls drew tight to his body as he pounded with more insistence, more need...just more.

She dragged her nails over his spine and kissed him with the fervor he never thought to know from his childhood friend. Yet here they were—in bed as though they never had a choice in the matter. Maybe all those years of friendship had been the true foreplay, and now there was no holding back.

He plunged in her walls. She clutched at him with her inner muscles. Soft moans rushed over his lips with her passionate display of kisses and finally, she took his hand and set it over her breast.

A rumble became a groan that grew into a growl. And he pinched her nipple as he thrust deep one last time. His orgasm shattered his self-control. He plundered her mouth while jets of cum shot into her.

He wanted her bareback.

He wanted her always.

Jesus, what put that thought into his head?

It fled as his balls emptied and her own release came hot on the heels of his.

"I feel...your cock...jerking inside me!" She squeezed her eyes shut and came, rocking upward, sliding over his length and taking all she needed from him.

Watching her face, he sucked in each small quiver of her lips and twitch of her eyelid as a final puff of a sigh burst out.

They collapsed together. For a solid minute, he only heard his own pounding heart. Then he heard hers and realized he'd dropped his head to rest on her breasts.

She cradled him against her with all the tenderness he never knew from a woman he slept with. It made the moment different.

It changed him.

After a long moment, she relaxed her thighs around his hips. "Ross..."

"Uh." He couldn't move even if she told him he was too heavy. The pillow of her soft breasts was home and a thousand emotions he couldn't name and never felt before.

"What is it, honey?" He waited for her to speak.

She wrapped her arms tight around him, making it impossible for him to move without peeling himself away from her.

"Can we... Can we do that again?"

His smile stretched across her damp skin. Then he moved to claim her lips, taking it from the top.

* * * * *

Ross's mouth on her breasts slowly leeched her mind out through her pores until she only cared about the exquisite pleasure.

His hot tongue roaming from nipple to nipple, sucking and gently biting set her on fire. Men hardly took time to make sure a lover gained pleasure. They hopped on and off with barely a kiss between. Not Ross.

He was better than anything she might have imagined. Even their first encounter in the motel left her partially aching. Now tingles spread through her, doubling and tripling as he kissed a path up her throat.

She arched her neck, and he crested over the point of her chin to capture her lips. They shared a moan, and she opened her eyes to stare at Ross.

Tenderness washed through his eyes. With her chest heaving to gain breath, she cupped his face, brushing her fingertips over his beard stubble.

"Close your eyes," he murmured in a rumble she felt to her curled toes.

Were they playing a trust game? She'd trust this man to catch her no matter what. He'd more than proved she could trust him with her life—and now her body.

She let her lids slip shut. Feeling him hovering above her, she waited with a breath catching in her throat.

Then he lightly pinched her chin and took her mouth. The gentle caress deepened. He pressed his tongue against her lips to seek entrance. She opened to him and he delved in, swirling against her tongue.

Suddenly, he withdrew. She started to open her eyes, but he stopped her with a command.

"Keep them shut."

Quivering with anticipation, she twisted her fingers in the sheets and waited for what he'd do.

His mouth landed on her shoulder. She turned her head, seeking him, but he was gone.

Next, he kissed her ribs just below her breast. Sucking in a gasp, she arched to find his lips — too late.

His teeth grazed her opposite hip. She expected him to continue lower, but he startled her by taking hold of her nipple in a suck that drew her off the bed. A louder moan escaped her, cut short when he released her nipple.

The bed shifted, and she tried to guess his position.

He sucked her toe into his mouth.

The warm, strange sensation never sounded exciting to her, but without her sense of sight, her nerve endings were short-circuiting. *Everything* felt amazing. Shocking.

She waited for a kiss to her ankle. Her knee. Neither came.

When something soft yet hard brushed over her mouth, she automatically snaked out her tongue. Salty-sweet juice hit her tastebuds. She gasped, and as soon as she opened, he slid his cock inside.

She blindly reached for him. Finding a muscled thigh, she dragged him closer, taking him deep in her throat. His roughened growl made her flames of desire leap. She had little experience giving oral, but she wanted to do this right for Ross. She wanted him to remember every single moment of her mouth on his cock.

Moaning around his thick length, she drew him in. He swayed out again until she could only lap at his swollen head. She felt a sticky string of precum stretch to the tip of her tongue.

"Don't move," he ground out. "Fuck, honey."

He moved again. She started to open her eyes, but his weight atop her felt so good, so drugging, that she couldn't if she tried. "I want you," he whispered against her lips.

"Take me," she urged.

"There's nothing I want more. But I only ever carry one condom."

She opened her eyes. His stare pierced through her, a knife blade of passion.

"Why?" she heard herself ask.

"I never want a woman more than once."

Her lips fell open, and his eyes creased at the corners with the strain of holding back mirrored in his tight mouth.

She placed her hands on his chest. His chest hair tickled her fingers, and his long cock lay heavy against her thigh, inches from her pussy.

She wanted him with a burning need that left her shaking. But she was aware of some pivot point between them. A tenuous struggle and a thread that if snapped, could never be rejoined.

He started to roll away from her, but she held him with a strength borne of her training in martial arts.

"Pip..." He shook his head.

She directed his gaze back to hers with a hand on his jaw. "We've already crossed lines."

"But this is too much. If I take you bare..." A shudder ripped through the planes of muscle on his spine.

She leaned up and kissed him, throwing every ounce of want into the caress. She wrapped her legs around his hips and rubbed her wet pussy against his length. If he chose to take this moment in another direction, she'd follow his lead.

For a heavy heartbeat, he froze over her. Letting her kiss him. A block of granite chiseled from his hometown of Stone Pass. She rubbed her aching clit against his hard shaft.

"Fuck!" He trapped her face in his hands and thrust his tongue over hers as he angled his cock toward her center. He entered her wet heat in one smooth glide that filled her, stretched her.

The insane feel of Ross bare inside her, with no barrier and only pure trust, tipped the scales in her mind—and the butterflies of young infatuation she harbored for Ross grew up into an adult love stronger than any other emotion she'd ever felt.

His groan vibrated through her. She opened her eyes to catch the look of absorption on his rugged features. Fiery sparks lit his green eyes like a wildfire overtaking a forest of pines.

Their mouths collided in time to their bodies. He meshed his fingers with hers and locked one hand to the bed. She jammed the fingers of her other hand into his hair, tugging him down again and again as he plundered her mouth.

His hard cock slipping through her clenching walls carried her to the brink. She felt wholly exposed—he knew her and she knew him.

It raised her up. Set her free. Any walls she ever hid behind crumbled.

Her orgasm struck with a blinding force. She felt the moment he threw it all away too as he stiffened, jerked once and then pumped his cum into her.

A dizzy realization that he could have just created a child with her, how irresponsible they were being, and how she didn't care at this moment because she

162

loved this man with a power that transcended life, all shattered with her release.

Waves of ecstasy pounded her. Ross's mouth snatched her cries.

She drew him close, and his strong arms held her through her final shudders.

With her body wrapped tight in his hold, he rolled them so she lay on top of him. Spent and breathing fast.

His rough hand stroking long swaths down her spine reinforced all the emotions whirling through her and made her know, without a doubt, they were real.

He pressed a kiss to her forehead. "I need to have a look at your laptop."

The last thing she expected to hear after mind-blowing sex—that came with a newfound feeling of love and topped off with a pregnancy risk—was about her laptop. It proved how far apart her mind was from Ross's.

Nodding, she disentangled herself from him and rolled off. His juices wet her inner thighs as the warmth of his body left her.

With a stiff spine, he walked completely naked to her bag. He set it on the table and unzipped it as if the faux leather contained a bomb.

She climbed off the bed, grabbed the closest garment—his shirt—and pulled it on. "You'll need my thumbprint."

"Let me get Silas on the phone. He's in charge of our cybersecurity division." He retrieved his phone and pulled his jeans on without underwear.

"It's me. I need you to hack Pippa's laptop."

She heard a low hoot coming from the phone. Ross's lips twitched but came short of forming a full smile at the obvious excitement projecting from his coworker at the prospect of hacking something.

Ross turned his attention to her. His gaze dropped over her front and his shirt she wore. "Okay, he says to open it and let him get a bead on the signals it's putting out."

"How can he do that?"

"I don't ask Silas about his magic. He wouldn't tell me if I did."

A bark of laughter projected from Ross's phone.

He held out his device toward the laptop.

"Sign in, he says," Ross instructed Pippa.

She threw a look at him and then entered the system using her thumbprint.

"There's more. Enter your password," Ross said.

When she angled her body to protect her code, he grabbed her shoulder and whipped her aside. "I'm not going to steal your secrets, Pippa. I almost got my ass shot off because of this fucking laptop."

"I thought you said they tracked me through my phone? And I don't like swiss cheese or relish having the same holes it does. Besides, I already have one gunshot wound, remember?" Ignoring the clawing urge to protect her passcode at all costs, she typed it in.

As the computer came to life, Ross listened to Silas speaking on the other end of the line. His lips grew grimmer as seconds ticked on.

"Well?" she burst out, unable to hold it in any longer.

He held up a finger for her to wait. She tapped her foot on the old motel carpet and studied his face. He drew the laptop closer to him and pressed a combination of keys. Immediately, the screen went black. Then numbers began to flash rapid-fire, blinking on and on while she stared in fear and amazement.

"I fucking knew it," Ross ground out.

She snapped her head around to stare at him.

"Disable it and trace it." A beat of silence. Then Ross said, "You got it? Good. Send me the report and get Landon and Mathias on it."

The Wyntons' cousins, who she'd met at a summer picnic or two over the years. They were cousins on his mother's side and were just as heartbreakingly handsome as the Wynton men, minus the dimples. She hadn't thought about them in years, but knowing they were working on something concerning her safety left her feeling protected from all sides.

"Thanks, Shanie. I'll be in touch." Ross hung up with Silas.

For a moment, he bowed his head over the laptop screen, which had gone back to its sign-in page. Her nerves pinged as she waited for him to speak.

When she couldn't take it another second, she said, "Well?"

"It's full of spyware. And worse." He raised his head and looked straight at her. "You didn't know your secure files are at risk?"

Ice-cold panic swept her. She sputtered, "Of course I didn't!"

"You're so smart, Pippa. How did you not know?"

"I'm smart in my field. And okay, some others like math. But I don't know computers. I just run what people set up for me."

"That's the issue. Someone is watching you."

"Have they breached my files?" She had passwords and fingerprint protection on each and every one, all different and more complex than the last.

"Not yet, but I'm sure they're trying to unlock them. We're going to remove the spies starting now." A dark red mottled his throat and climbed into his face.

She took in the banked fury in his eyes too. "You're going to have a stroke if you don't calm down. Your blood pressure is sky high."

He slanted a glance at her.

"I'm serious. We're going to…" Going down on him right now would only make his system more haywire. Inspiration struck. "We're going to meditate."

He widened his stance. "What?"

"Meditate."

"I don't buy into that mumbo-jumbo."

"It's not mumbo-jumbo. It actually helps calm people down, and right now, you and I can both use it. Come on." She grabbed the sheet off the bed and spread it on the floor with one shake. Then she pointed at it. "Sit."

He reluctantly took a step onto the sheet. She led by example, sitting cross-legged on the floor. Drawing in a deep breath, she tried to find her center. When she realized Ross wasn't sitting, she looked up at him.

He heaved a sigh and sat next to her, copying her pose. "This is the last thing I should be doing right now," he muttered.

"Self-care is important. Now fold your hands in your lap." She showed him, and he imitated her. "Close your eyes and breathe in through your nose to three counts. Good. Now exhale to three."

Five breaths in she got that prickle on her skin that told her that he was staring at her. She opened her eyes and sure enough, he wasn't meditating, only staring.

"You can't relax if you don't try, Ross."

"Who says looking at you isn't relaxing? Where did you learn this anyway?"

"Tibet. I spent some time there as well."

"Of course you did." He lowered his gaze to her bare thighs.

Her stomach leaped with awareness. They'd just had insanely hot sex — twice. And she sat inches from the man she wanted, wearing nothing but his shirt.

"Hell, don't give me that look," he said.

"What look?"

"The one that says you want me buried in your pussy again."

She shivered.

The monks would scold her for her meditation breathing.

Chapter Ten

Everything about Pippa called to Ross to drop his jeans and claim her again. But he needed to focus first, and he couldn't do that with her nearby.

"Why don't you take a shower? I'm going to make some phone calls." He was changing the subject from sex because if he didn't, they'd never leave this room. And eventually, the people after her would catch up with them.

Her expression fell, but she nodded. He watched her stand and grab her bag before entering the bathroom. Once the door closed, he got up.

Pacing the small room wouldn't give his brain enough space to work out the issues at hand—he needed acres of ranch for that—but a tiny motel room off the beaten path was all he could manage for now.

The shower started behind the door when he paced by. Window. Door. Picture of bear cubs.

As he passed the table, he glared at the laptop. He didn't understand every detail concerning the spyware on her computer, but Silas told him it was bad and the evil fingers went deep. Whoever had

169

placed it in her system hadn't yet breached her files containing the genetic editing research she did. But they were close.

Knowing she couldn't overhear him with the water running, he walked to the window and looked out on the stark landscape as he added his entire team to a group call.

Boone picked up first, and Josiah and Noah clicked in after that.

Silas said, "What's up? I'm pretty busy cleaning your girlfriend's computer."

Ross swiped a hand over his face, battling the word *girlfriend*. The statement hit home hard. What was Pippa to him?

She was dear to him. Always had been, from the time they met as kids. She was someone he looked forward to talking to and watching her grow her skills on the ranch or with the flyrod.

Landon and Mathias responded to the call, and Ross took a moment to gather his thoughts.

"Ross? You good, bro?" Boone drawled.

"Yeah. I'm thinkin' about Seattle. I know I said we need to lay a trap there, but now I'm second-guessing that decision."

"Did something else happen?" Concern came off as a rougher edge to Boone's voice.

"No. We're safe for the moment, and I've got Roman on my six. But the convention's a big security risk I'm not sure we're ready to handle."

"We're ready," Josiah said with conviction ringing in his tone. "We've worked bigger venues. Remember the size of that crowd during the riot outside Denver? We handled that shit—we can do this convention."

He considered all the options. He had to think of Pippa—she came first.

"Let's talk through every angle. This is our roundtable right now." An image of them in their white hats, circling the conference table back on the ranch, filtered into his mind.

Josiah sent them a diagram of the conference center, and they discussed areas of concern. They agreed to keep Pippa from her family's house and to place two unmarked cars on their street in case.

Talk turned to the shootout on the highway.

"I ran that plate you gave me, Ross. Get this—it isn't even real," Josiah told him.

He paced to the table, listening for the water to shut off in the bathroom. "What do you mean?"

"Someone created a fake plate."

"That sounds like a whole other investigation to me," Noah added.

"But not our problem right now. Did the police ID the men after they were recovered from the wrecks?"

"No word on that as of yet, boss. I'll keep you updated. Whoever is after Pippa has enough money and resources to hire outside help."

"Run financials on every person on the list, Josiah."

"I'm ahead of you. Nothing's come up as of yet."

Boone spoke up, "We're just glad you had Roman with you."

"Yeah, we're going to send The Guard a big fucking thank-you barrel of whiskey for their help. If Roman hadn't been on that road, Pippa and I would be dead. Or I would be and she'd be kidnapped." His throat clamped off for a moment. He pinched the bridge of his nose and fought through the emotions that statement raised in him.

He couldn't lose her to these assholes.

"Let's dig deeper. What else can we find, maybe through her computer risk? I want names. Then every one of you is going to interrogate someone on that list I gave you."

"Got it, Ross. I'm sending the names to everyone now."

"Thanks, Josiah." His tone was steeped in warmth for his team. He started to ask Boone about the possibility of reaching Seattle sooner to scope out the hotel where he'd keep Pippa safeguarded, when the shower shut off.

Knowing she might overhear, he pitched his voice low. "Keep vigilant, men. I'll be in touch."

When Pippa opened the door, he was digging in his bag for clean clothes. He dropped his bag of toiletries to the bed and looked up at her.

She'd removed his shirt, and damn if he didn't miss seeing how it hung around her long, naked thighs. Her wet hair dipped over her shoulders to dampen her clean top. "Shower pressure's not that great, but the water's hot."

He nodded. "I'll shower in a minute. I need to talk to you."

Her eyes widened a fraction as she crossed the room. When he caught a whiff of her body wash, his insides gripped with desire.

"Sit down."

She arched a brow. "I have a feeling this is a standing moment. I think better on my feet."

"I can relate. Okay, I'll say it plain. I'm not sure we're going to Seattle."

She blinked. "You said you're going to draw out the person who's after me."

"I'm not sure it's the right move. We're analyzing the situation, but fact is, you might miss that conference, Pip."

He expected her to give a stoic nod, the way she always did and always had as a child when told she couldn't do something.

But she whirled on him, face alight with anger. "No." She slashed a hand through the air between them. "I'm not missing that conference. There's a lot riding on my speech. I'm not only delivering hope to an entire room full of people who this subject matters to. I'm giving hope to the *world*."

173

Stunned by the emotion and strength in her voice, he could only stare at her. This was a side of Pippa he'd never seen before.

"This is huge to me, Ross. And you know how important careers are to people like us."

They were more alike than he ever thought.

He steeled his thighs to keep from going to her and pulling her into his arms. Why hadn't he seen it before? Because she was city and he was country. She was book-smart and he had common sense. Despite these variations, when he looked into her eyes he saw she was right.

Their core values and their upbringings were only a small portion of that similarity. She'd grown into a strong and capable woman with enough brains to turn him on just as much as the body she'd morphed into. They were both driven...and they were in this together.

His phone buzzed. Still holding her gaze, he brought it to his ear.

"Ross, we need Pippa to sign in. She just received an email I think might be of interest to you."

Heart in his throat, he hurled himself the few steps across the worn carpet to the laptop. He caught her by the wrist and dragged her to the table. She gulped off a cry of surprise as they stopped before the computer.

"Josiah says to sign in. You got an email."

Staring at the device, she lifted her fingers and dug them into her hair. He shot a glance at her face and saw fear spelled across her beautiful features.

It tore at his heart.

Hooking an arm around her waist, he reeled her into his arms. She dropped her forehead to his chest. "It's all right, honey," he said gruffly.

"Uh...thanks?" Josiah was still on the line.

"Not you, dickhead."

Josiah cracked up laughing.

He wanted to hang up on his brother, but he needed the information he provided too.

Smoothing his hand over Pippa's damp hair, he said, "It's no big deal. Just sign in and read the email."

When she raised her eyes to his, the pain he saw reflected in the depths struck him in the gut this time.

"What if I learn someone I trust...someone I enjoy being around...wants me dead?"

He didn't tell her that was *exactly* what she'd find out eventually. Someone she knew and trusted betrayed her.

"You can do this, Pippa. Come on." He gently turned her to face the laptop. She stood still for a long moment and then jerked into action and entered her login.

"That isn't the same passcode you entered before," he said.

"I have a different one for emails. Lots of levels of security in this system."

"Are you hearing this?" he asked Josiah.

"I'm *seeing* it. It's state of the art, I'll give MIZR credit for that. Has she reached her emails yet?"

"There are so many," she said, scrolling through the inbox. "I'll have to read them all, since I have no idea what I need to see."

Starting at the top, she skimmed the post about a special lunch for a lab assistant's birthday. She went to the next. This from her friend Meredith. A photo of a flower bloomed on the screen along with a GET WELL SOON beneath it. Seven heart emojis followed and then Meredith's name.

"That was sweet of her," Pippa said softly before moving to the next email.

A few came from people she'd never mentioned, containing in-depth science terms. Just reading it over her shoulder dulled Ross to pieces. When she hit the next email, a name flashed up that she'd mentioned. A name they were investigating.

"Josiah, is it the email from Ryan Letters?"

"That's the one."

She threw Ross a sideways glance. Was that a blush climbing her cheeks?

"Open it," he commanded in a tight voice.

Together, they silently read the email, which was only partly about work. The rest seemed pretty damn personal to Ross.

She moved to the next. He stopped her with a hand on her arm.

"I don't see anything untoward in that email. No clues that Ryan wants me dead." Defiance lit her eyes.

"He likes you."

"You're insane."

"He wants to jump you."

"Don't be crass. And you're wrong."

"Am I? *'We can hit the research as soon as you feel better,'*" he mimicked from the email.

"Yeah—he meant exactly that. We can continue work as soon as I'm back in the lab."

"'I missed seeing you in the lunchroom.'"

She shrugged. "So? Ryan's got a girlfriend. He isn't interested in me, and I only like his mind."

Ross leveled his stare at her.

"Ross...I knew this would happen. You're only acting this way because we slept together!"

"Hooooeeeee," Josiah sang into Ross's ear.

He ended the call and slammed the phone on the table. Taking a step closer to Pippa, he forced her to back up. "In five seconds, all of my brothers—probably my sister too—will know what happened between us. And no—I'm not suspicious of Ryan Letters because I had my hands and tongue all over your body."

She shuddered.

177

"It's because he's dropping lines in that email that are red alerts to people like me and my team. If he likes you, he has a reason to stalk you. If he harbors professional jealousy of your brain and talent and your find, then he has a motive to come after you."

She shook her head. "I don't understand. He likes me but he's jealous? Those ideas completely conflict with each other."

"Not if you've studied criminal minds, and I have. He may have an unhealthy attraction to you."

"You're wrong."

"Envy drives most people."

"It doesn't drive me."

"I know, honey. Me either. But I want you to search your mind and tell me every single detail about this guy. I don't care if it was a weird feeling you got from him or a certain look."

She gazed at Ross for a long minute and finally nodded. "Okay. But I can't work without food, Ross."

His mind tripped over the off-topic statement.

"What are you getting us for dinner?" she demanded.

His lips quirked. "Of all the things I expected you to say, this was the furthest from my mind. Though I don't know why it surprises me from a woman who would eat the last blueberry bar."

* * * * *

"That tasted better than it actually was because I was so hungry." Pippa sat back in the stiff chair and clasped her hands over her stomach.

Across the table, Ross stuck an entire chicken wing in his mouth, clamped his teeth and pulled the bone from his mouth clean of meat. She watched him do that three more times before he tossed the last chicken wing into the paper tray.

"Everything's better when you haven't eaten in a while."

She studied him. He'd showered and changed clothes. He wore his chambray shirt open at the throat, showing off his tanned skin as well as a few hairs creeping up from his chest. Veins snaked down his forearms, visible below his rolled sleeves. Even without his hat, he still owned the cowboy look one hundred percent.

"What would you eat if you could pick the menu?" she asked.

He cut a glance at her and wiped his mouth with a paper napkin in a manly move that would leave a woman breathless.

"Ribeye and baked potato with sour cream and loads of butter. My momma's rolls." He groaned.

She did too. "I remember your momma's rolls well. I helped her make them once, but I've never attempted it on my own. My mother made them once for Easter and they came out like stones. We still tease her about it."

His smile popped the dimple in his cheek. "What would you eat?"

"Doritos."

He chuckled. "You? Junk food? Doesn't the fake cheese alter your genetic makeup or something?"

She laughed. "That's not how it works."

"I saw a vending machine at the end of the building. I can have Roman grab you a bag if you want."

"No, I'm full. Thank you, though." Their gazes caught and held. The touch of his eyes roaming over her face, hair and down to her breasts left her with a burning memory of his rough hands on her.

His tongue on her.

"We're leaving at four a.m. Roman and I decided it's best to travel at a quiet time of day."

She dragged in a breath, the warm fuzzies in her stomach forgotten. "So we really are going to Seattle?"

He nodded. "The guys and I worked it out. Boone's left his current post and is on his way there now to secure things the best he can for our arrival. The rest get into Seattle right before we do."

Looking down at her twisted fingers, she tried to picture what could happen in Seattle. She couldn't, so she gave up trying. She met Ross's stare. "Your mom told me she worries about you all doing this dangerous work. If she knew what happened to us so far, she'd lock you in your room."

"I have no doubt she could too. Pippa, it's been decided that you can't go to your family's house. We'll have guards on them, just in case. But we can't take the risk."

She blew out a sigh. "Even though I already knew it, I still held some hope of seeing them."

"I'm sorry."

"C'est la vie," she said with a forced note of brightness.

He tipped his head, eyes glowing at her. "I suppose you studied in France too."

"No. I only spent one weekend there. Meredith and I took a long weekend after we graduated from our doctorate program."

"I wasn't aware you graduated together."

"Yes. We started MIZR at the same time, though I'd been slated to work there since I won the science competition in high school."

"Did you get her a job there?"

Surprise made her blink in reaction. "No. Not at all. She's brilliant. She's done a lot of work on fusion proteins."

"Whatever those are."

She chuckled. In only a few days her voice had returned to normal and the bruising on her throat began to fade. "Tell me your hopes for WEST Protection."

He squared his shoulders, making them appear broader. "I want to be the best in the country."

"I have complete faith in your skills."

As their gazes locked, it hit her — how different their lives were. She worked in a lab and was happy as a cell organelle to bury her nose in research and learning. Ross lived and breathed the ranch and his security company. They lived states apart. Seeing each other in future would be impossible.

None of these revelations shocked her, but they did jab her square in the heart. Anything they may have gained would be lost. Cut short. Maybe forgotten.

No, she'd never forget their scorching encounters and his burning kisses. Even the way he looked at her now left her on edge and breathless.

"I don't know what you're thinking, Pip, but I don't like the look on your face." His voice came out as a low rasp.

She turned her attention to her hands. "I was just thinking of my family. How much I miss them."

When she glanced up, she found him studying her. Since she was a terrible liar, she wouldn't be surprised if he called her out on the one she'd just told. But he remained silent, and the moment passed.

"How do you manage to throw yourself into the protection agency and keep up with the ranch?" Turning the topic seemed to be her go-to when it came to avoiding strained moments with Ross.

Thankfully, he rolled with it. "We've got enough ranch hands. Most of what I do is on the management end. I'm slowly taking over some of those jobs my dad always did."

"Is he ready to retire?"

"Don't know if he'll ever fully retire. But I think he's happy to step back sometimes and let us do the work. Pretty sure he always liked bossing us around better."

She smiled. "That's what they call a supervisor. And you're the same, Ross. Cut from the same bolt of worn denim."

Her statement made him drop his gaze. For a moment, she wondered if she'd offended him in some way. Then he said, "Ryan Letters split with his girlfriend three weeks ago."

Her jaw dropped. "He didn't say anything to me."

"Would he have said something? You say you aren't close."

"We aren't. It's office chit-chat. Water cooler talk. I know he roots for Detroit Mercy Titans basketball and he and his girlfriend were talking about getting a place together."

"What does he know about you?"

Flustered, she straightened in her seat. The angle of the back was starting to make her spine ache the longer she sat here, but their discussion wasn't finished, and moving to the bed meant other things might happen. Things she wanted with every burning ember of her being.

But whatever chemistry boiled between them would end abruptly the minute the danger ended and they returned to their separate lives.

Another pang hit her heart—sharper than before.

"Ryan doesn't know anything about me."

"Does he know what team you root for?"

Irritated, she turned the question on him. "Do you?"

He leaned forward, staring her in the eyes. "You hate basketball."

"So do you." Why was her heart thumping so hard and fast? Knowing some stupid little detail about her such as the fact she wasn't a sports fan meant nothing.

He did know what made her moan, though. How to make her pant for more.

And she knew how to raise his skin into goosebumps under her fingertips.

That bolt of lightning that she really did love Ross sent electricity through her limbs. Energized, she pushed away from the table.

"If you suspect Ryan has something to do with the situation I'm in, then investigate it. By all means, arrest him. If he deserves it, if he chose this path. But please don't suggest that something more lies between us. We work together. Nothing more."

She stood and started by him to the bed. As she passed, he thrust out his arm to bar her way. She glanced down at the obstruction, passion raging through her veins. She wanted to turn into his arms. She wanted to run away.

Closing her eyes for a beat, she said, "It's late, Ross. I'm tired."

When she opened her eyes again, he'd withdrawn his arm.

"I'd like to talk to my family. Am I allowed to video call them on my laptop?"

He reached into his breast pocket and pulled out his phone. She stared at the device dwarfed by the size of his big, deliciously rough palm. "Use mine."

"What if you get a call while I'm on?"

"It will go to voicemail."

She took the phone from him, trying not to brush her fingers against his skin. She crossed to the bed and sank to the edge. For long minutes, she didn't dial her parents' number or Holly's. The room felt like a cage locking her within its walls. When would this all end? Did she clue her family in to the peril she faced?

Across the room, Ross's chair creaked as he shifted to his feet and began clearing the detritus of their meal. She stared at him for a heartbeat, unable to imagine being ripped from him.

Would her life be enough once she returned to it? When compared to her dull existence — she could only think of it this way now—she didn't know if she could ever be happy without Ross.

Swallowing the lump in her throat, she dialed her parents instead of video calling. She didn't trust herself to keep the stress off her face.

The minute her mother's voice projected into her ear, the blockage in her throat slipped downward into her stomach and lay there, a heavy coal.

"Pippa! Hold on. Let me get your father. Gabriel! We're so glad to hear from you." She pictured her momma's beaming expression and her father's wide grin and ached for them all the more.

Forcing a note of normalcy into her tone, she said, "Hi, Mom and Dad."

From the corner of her eye, she took note of Ross dumping the garbage into the small trash can in the corner of the room. He kept his face in profile so she couldn't tell his reaction.

She was more than out of her element with the hot cowboy bodyguard listening to her every word and watching her every move.

"We're all ready to pick you up at the airport. Same time? They didn't change your flight time, did they?" Her father's question didn't surprise her. He was always a stickler for an itinerary.

She struggled with words—with that lump in her throat too. The one that threatened a long, draining bout of tears.

"Um...I had a change of plans."

Ross's head jerked up.

"I'm not flying into Seattle. I'm...I'm with Ross."

Silence met her statement.

"Ross Wynton! Do you mean Ross Wynton?" her mother asked.

"Yes, that Ross."

He turned to look at her, but she skittered her gaze to the side.

"Why are you with Ross, dear?"

"We just...ran into each other." Lying to her parents would surely earn her a spanking? Or at least time-out in the corner.

"How exciting! Where did you run into him?"

"It's a long story," she evaded the question. "But he's traveling with me. We're in his truck."

He didn't move from where he stood. In fact, his muscled body appeared hardened, his stance wide and braced for impact.

"Well, we know that you're in good hands then. We haven't seen Ross in a couple years. He was away doing a training last time we visited the Wyntons. Such a driven young man, and an enormous help around the Wynton Ranch, according to his family." Her mother did most of the talking, as usual, while her father provided grunts of agreement.

"Yes, he is."

Ross's gaze sharpened on her.

187

"I suppose he'll be with you when you come home, and we've got plenty of room," her mother said.

"I don't know if he can stay." The sadness weighting her down finally seeped into her voice. She cleared her throat and tried to cover what she'd said so her parents didn't read into anything. "He has his own work to see to."

"Of course, he's so busy. But surely he has time for old friends."

"I'll ask him, but we can't make any promises. Well, it's late. I'm going to catch some sleep, and you should too."

"We'll see you soon, Pippa. Love you." Her dad's declaration finally broke the dam of tears free.

Biting back a cry, she nodded first and then realized they couldn't see her. She sucked in a breath. "I love you too. Night, Mom. Night, Dad."

She dropped the phone to her lap and lowered her face into her hands. Tears wet her fingers, hot and unstoppable. The bed dipped under Ross's weight. He slid his arm around her shoulders, turning her against him. When her body gave a shaking heave, he made a noise in his chest.

"Damn, honey. Come here." He pulled her into his lap.

The only place she wanted to be.

In the end, when she was safe and this was all over, letting go of her cowboy bodyguard would be the thing to finally break her.

Chapter Eleven

Ross glared at the whiteout of snow in front of the truck. "The last thing we need is more bad weather."

"I ate all the blueberry bars. We're down to water now."

She didn't sound a bit fussed about being stuck on the road in a blizzard for the second time that week.

He growled with annoyance at the situation. "Slowing down means the people hunting you have time to catch up."

"I don't have my phone anymore. And you said that Silas removed the spyware from my laptop overnight."

"He did." Ross laid awake half the night, grabbing sleep in twenty-minute spells, alternately battling his throbbing hard-on and the need to stand guard over Pippa.

He slapped the wheel. "Dammit! Why did they have to shut down the road between exits? There's nowhere to get off."

"I have to be at the conference soon for check-in. I know you don't want to reach Seattle, but I didn't know you have so much command that you can call down snow and keep me away."

He stared at her and then dropped his gaze to her mouth. Plump. Sweet. She could suck cock like a courtesan and twist him up in knots with her sassy comebacks.

"Shush, woman."

She geared up to say more, and he reached over, looped his hand around her nape and dragged her mouth to his. She gave in immediately to the crush of his lips. The instant she went boneless, he deepened the kiss by gliding his tongue over hers.

She moaned. So did he.

She unbuckled her seatbelt, and he did the same.

"As long as we're at a standstill, we might as well make good use of our time," she murmured between sweeping passes of his tongue.

Suddenly, she threw herself over the console into his lap. His cock responded with a jolt of anticipation. Clamping his hands on her waist, he dragged her over his groin. They shared a roughened groan that mingled with the wind howling at gale force outside the vehicle.

Bracketing his face with her hands, she leaned into him for another kiss. Her honey sweetness stole his mind. So responsive. So right.

Long moments stretched on while he plundered her, taking the kiss from intense to gentle and back again.

She broke apart. "Why didn't you take me last night?"

He'd been asking himself the same question since the minute she climbed between the sheets. One look at the curve of her hip under the covers had him grinding his teeth. He could have reached out and had her melting in his arms within seconds. Yet, he held back.

Instead, he lay staring at the yellowed ceiling thinking about getting her home to her family, if not this weekend then someday soon. But each time he touched on the idea of her returning to work in Detroit—alone—it felt like he poked at a sore tooth. And he didn't like pain.

In the end, he lay stiff beside her. Touching her would both ease his torment and incite more pain when they parted. She was smart—she knew their time together would end.

"Maybe we're not meant to go to Seattle," she whispered an inch from his lips.

He nodded. "Maybe it's fate."

"Events developing outside a person's control," she said as if quoting from a dictionary buried in the depths of her mind.

He slammed his mouth over hers. Wind, snow and ice drummed at the truck. They were in a dangerous situation he feared he wouldn't get her out of. Yet kissing her seemed to be the only solution right now.

When they tore away again, she searched his face. He pressed his lips to her forehead, drinking in her scent and committing it to memory.

Looking over her head at the windows they'd steamed up with their increased body heat, he experienced a sharp pull on his heart.

"Pippa—"

She tipped her face up to his.

Her beautiful eyes captured his heart.

"I... I don't want to let you go after this. I..." The words swirled in his mind and edged to his lips. "I love you," he grated out.

The lights in her eyes cooled and then dimmed. She stiffened in his arms before clambering out of his lap. She hit the passenger seat, her head twisted to the side window so he saw only the back of her head.

He lifted a shaky hand and pulled off his hat. Fuck. What just happened? Didn't women want declarations of love? When she looked at him, he swore he read the same thing on her face. Had he completely misread her?

Tense silence filled the truck, equal to the weight of being held at gunpoint. Neither of them spoke. Minutes ticked by. To avoid looking at her, he glanced at the gas gauge and saw it dropping. Cutting the engine would mean they'd lose precious time if they had to find a quick escape. But they couldn't go anywhere without gas.

He'd never confessed his love before. Well, not since third grade when Amanda Grace Richards gave him a pink paper heart on Valentine's Day. To finally say the words and receive only silence in response had him swerving between confused and pissed off.

Should he say something else to cover it up? And why the hell didn't she love him too? Her body reacted to his every look and touch. She laughed at all his jokes. When she told him she didn't have any interest in Ryan Letters, he believed her. If there wasn't someone else, then what stopped her from having feelings for him?

"Dammit," he said under his breath. Her shoulder tensed but she didn't turn.

Turning his worries to her safety, he withdrew his phone and called Roman to ask if he could see anything and received a joking reply that he was a whole twelve feet in front of them and their angles were the same.

Then he called Josiah, who told him the calf was doing better and it would most likely live. Also, Boone had reached Seattle and was now networking with security at the hotel and conference center. These small discussions didn't help his mood or distract him from the mute woman seated beside him.

"I found something in Pippa's spam folder, too," Josiah said.

194

Clutching the phone to his ear, he waited for more.

"An email that bounced between about ten different IP addresses. It could be nothing — or it could be something."

"Forward it to me and I'll take a look. Did you run it past Shanie?" he referred to Silas by his last name.

"Yup. He thinks it might hold some weight in this case too."

After he ended the call, he sent a sidelong look at Pippa's ramrod-stiff spine.

"Pippa — "

She twisted in her seat to face the front. "What did Josiah say?"

In total Pippa Hamlin style, she changed the subject. What choice did he have but to roll with it? He wasn't about to argue about love, and he wouldn't say it a second time.

"They discovered something in your spam folder they want me to have a look at." They didn't look at each other, which had his blood boiling in his veins. Minutes before, she rubbed her pussy on his cock and kissed him like she meant it. Now she was ice-cold.

Maybe she didn't want more than sex from him, and he'd crossed that line. In this scenario, he was taking the typical role of the female who wanted more than the man did. Now he saw why some women hated on men.

195

He flipped up the screen containing the email.

"Well?" she asked. "What is it?"

He gave a slow shake of his head. "It doesn't appear to be spam to me. It looks like it came through the chain of command at MIZR."

She finally turned her head to pierce him in her gaze. "I don't know how it's possible I'd miss something associated with my company. Everything comes through a filter but doesn't go to spam."

"I think this might be why." He held up the phone for her to read.

As her gaze moved down the screen, they widened until the whites showed around the hazel irises. "Oh my God." Her voice rasped with fear. Over their days together, her voice had grown clearer, healing from her injury. But it still held a womanly husk that echoed like a gong inside him. Now, the throatiness returned full force.

She reached as if to snatch the phone from him but dropped her hand to her lap. Her fingers clamped on her leg until the knuckles turned white. "Someone offered me money for my breakthrough?"

"Looks that way."

"MIZR doesn't operate that way."

"Seems as if someone is acting on his own. And he has enough money behind him to pay you a lump sum of twenty-five million dollars."

"That's..." She broke off, shaking her head. "It has to be a scam. One of those men from Europe who found my name in his mother's will and is going to send me the inheritance if I provide him with my bank account number."

"I don't think so, Pippa."

When she met his stare, he saw shock mingled with sadness there. "You're suggesting someone in MIZR offered to pay me off and when I didn't respond to that email, they turned to hunting me for it?"

Pain pulsed in her tone. Her eyes flooded with tears, causing them to sparkle brighter. He could be an asshole and hold back any comfort he could give her because she didn't return his feelings. But he would never do that.

"I'm sorry, honey. C'mere." He reached out for her and pulled her into his arms. She rested her head on his chest, and he waited to hear the hitching sounds of her crying, but when he glanced down at her, he found her cheeks dry.

She didn't make a move to slide into her seat. In fact, she seemed pretty damn content to be curled against his chest as she processed the new clue as to who could want her dead.

Even if she didn't love him in return, she did want his support.

And he loved her enough to provide everything she needed and then some.

"Ross."

"Yes?"

"I need you to do something for me."

"Anything."

"I want you to get me a weapon. Because I'm not going into that conference center unarmed."

By now, he shouldn't be surprised by anything she said or did. The woman had more ability than some security officers or prison guards he'd met.

"I'm not going to ask if you know how to shoot. I know your father would have taken you to the range."

"Yes. He's an outdoorsman, and he taught me everything he knows."

"I can't give you a weapon, Pippa. I can't put you at more risk. You asked me to protect you—now trust me that I will."

A shiver shook her, and he tightened his arms to safeguard her from the worst of the storm.

"If it really is someone who heads MIZR—and I can't imagine who else would have that kind of money—then I feel I've lost everything."

"What do you mean?" He smoothed his hand over her silky hair.

"I've believed in this company since I was a teen, when they paid for my way through college and to get me through a doctorate degree in trade for working for them." She lifted her head and looked at Ross. "I feel like a sow that's been fattened up for market. They gave me every opportunity to learn. For them. They trained me and provided me with the facility to discover this thing that will change the world. Now they want to pay me off or kill me to get it. Well, I'm not giving up my secrets, and I'm willing to die to keep it out of their hands."

He closed his eyes on her forceful oath. "You won't have to, Pippa. Because I will."

* * * * *

Pippa felt as though someone had clubbed her over the head and dragged her into a pitch-black cave. No light shed on the problems she was facing. And no shadows meant she didn't know what to hide from.

There was also the huge problem of Ross.

His declaration of love blindsided her—shocked her to the depths of her soul. It was the only thing she wanted to hear from the man, and yet it terrified her. Their lives were too different, and loving each other only complicated things more.

He was married to his work. She was too. Yes, they were so alike it was scary. That should give her some hope that her feelings could actually go somewhere, but she knew better. What was she going to do? Give up her important life's work, a life she was willing to sacrifice in order to share her finds with the world on her own terms, so she could live on the Wynton Ranch and support Ross's dreams?

Not that she didn't care about his dreams—far from it. The edges of their universes hardly touched, though.

The Seattle hotel felt cold and without personality after the motels they'd stayed in on their journey. The four white walls, king-sized bed piled with pristine white bed linens and down pillows, and the stark modern furniture in the room had nothing on those bear cubs playing in a creek on the motel wall.

She was also alone. Ross had installed her in this room with her bag and a promise that he or one of his team would be outside her door at all times. After the closeness they'd shared of hours in the truck, being alone left her hollow.

On those miles of road, they'd shared so much of themselves. They'd been trapped in two whiteouts. Been shot at and hunted down. But she'd been alive.

Coming from a sterile lab and now being dropped in this lonely white room, she had to ask herself how she'd journeyed so far from the things she loved. The outdoors. Her family. Ross's family. Personal connections. The one person she managed to retain a relationship with was Meredith, and she was lucky to have her. She hoped her evasive responses to Meredith's kindness over the past few days hadn't pushed her friend away too.

Her room towered over Seattle, and she had a great view of the skyline. She also had a wall of glass doors leading to a private balcony. Growing up in Seattle, she knew the weather fluctuated all over the place at this time of year, but suddenly she wanted nothing more than some fresh air.

She walked to the French doors, but stopped short of touching the handle. Ross told her not to go out there alone. At the time, she asked how anybody would get to her so high and with huge spans between her and the next balcony, but he only gave her that hard look that brooked no arguments.

Turning from the balcony, she looked at the other set of glass doors, these partitioning off the bathroom suite from the rest of the space. She already had a shower today, but maybe a nice soak in a hot bath would ease her nerves and help the icy cold dread of what would come in the morning when she took that podium as keynote speaker.

Right this second, Ross was organizing an army of security to protect her. But she'd studied too much about security breaches in American history—just looking at the US Presidents. Things could slip.

She walked through the glass doors and locked them behind her. Then she paused at the long teakwood vanity to pull the elastic out of her hair. From beyond the glass, she heard a knock on the outer door. She was too exhausted to deal with more information Ross would give her about MIZR or her colleagues, so she ignored the sound.

He knocked more insistently until he pounded the door.

She turned from the vanity to face the entrance as it burst inward. Ross stood there like a brick wall, head jerking right and left in search of her. Her heart tripped as his stare landed on her.

Through the glass, she saw raw desire spelled over his rugged features. She sucked in a sharp gasp. When she backed up a step, she hit the vanity.

He took a step toward the doors, muscles rolling, the denim pulling taut over his chiseled thighs and his fists curled.

Giving herself up to him now would tear her apart. Her heart already halfway belonged to him—if he took her body right this minute, she'd give up her entire soul.

As she watched him cross the white carpet, his cowboy boots leaving divots in the plush fibers with each stride, she started to shake.

She wanted him. All she had to do was open the door and invite him in.

He already loves me.

She clasped the vanity to keep from going to him.

"Pippa." He peered through the glass at her.

Her gaze dipped to his chest that pillowed her head so perfectly to the front of his jeans. His erection swelled his fly outward. Shivers hit her core, and her nipples hardened in reaction.

If she let him in, would she win or lose? Would she give up or gain everything?

She swallowed hard as their gazes locked once more.

His jaw firmed, and he reached out to a nearby table, ripped the heavy stone lamp off it, tearing the cord from the wall, and smashed it through the door.

She cried out as glass shattered. Ross stepped through it as though he walked through a wall of cloud. In two steps, he grabbed her into his arms and kissed her, whirling to set her on the vanity with her legs spread to fit his muscled hips as he claimed her mouth, her senses, her heart, in one scorching kiss.

He straightened to stare at her. "Don't try to hide from me. You can't."

Raising trembling fingers to his chiseled jaw, she whispered, "No, I can't. I need you, Ross."

"Damn right you do." He swooped in, slamming his mouth over hers. She moaned in surrender as he lifted her, crunched through the glass shards to the bed and lay her down. Following her with his body, his chest heaved against hers.

"Say it, Pippa. I can see it in your eyes."

Could she? They were only words, right? They weren't vows, and she could still walk away afterward.

A voice deep in her mind gave a short, dry laugh. *Go ahead and try.*

His jaw firmed more and his eyes glittered with what appeared to be banked anger. "Say. The. Words."

She gulped. "Ross, I… I…"

Say it.

"I love you."

His eyelids slipped shut and when he opened them again, intense love poured from his green gaze.

When he lowered his lips to hers, a new tenderness leaped between them.

Passion rose inside her. Locking her legs around his hips, she dragged him down so his weight pinned her. Need hummed through her veins, flickering hotter with each stroke of his tongue.

In a swift jerk, he removed her top. Finding her braless, he let out a groan a split second before he leaned in and lightly grazed her right nipple. She arched, and he bit her left. The dark need his love bites rose inside her shook her to the core.

She yanked at his shirt buttons. When she issued a noise of frustration, he took over. She shoved off her jeans and panties and then reached for his belt.

Slipping a hand under her nape and one beneath her ass, he drew her into his lips and cock. She melted at the passion transmitting into their kiss, combusted at the way he lifted her into him again and again until she thought she'd die from the pressure.

She tugged at his hair. He buried his face against her neck, kissing and licking her to a frenzy. As if him hurling a lamp through the glass door in order to reach her hadn't already done enough to turn her on.

With pulling and tugging, she managed to unzip his fly and draw his thick length into her hand. As she stroked the velvet steel, he let out a wild growl that sent goosebumps skittering over her flesh. Panting, she stroked him even as she worked his jeans down his hips on one side.

He leaned onto one arm to help her. Thrusting her hips up, she begged him with her eyes.

"Nothing could stop me," he ground out. He fit the head of his cock at her slick core and filled her in one smooth stroke.

Buried to the balls.

She cried out, gripping his shoulders for leverage. She wanted more. All of him.

She needed to hear him say it again.

"Ross!" Catching his face in her hands, she met his stare.

He stilled.

"I'm in love with you."

"I'm so in love with you." The moon and stars hung in his eyes as he leaned down and kissed her, taking their frenzied lovemaking to the next level.

Chapter Twelve

An animal need to hear Pippa screaming his name melded with his warrior's desire to kill for her. Whatever magic lived in those three little words — *I love you* — stole the rest of his heart and made it hers.

She gripped her inner walls with a tight hold as he drove into her body. A tight knot stretched to the breaking point, but he held back. He couldn't end this yet. Deep inside, he knew this moment would free them both.

When she scored her nails lightly over his spine, a low rumble vibrated through him. He had to take her every way. Everywhere. Now.

Withdrawing, he flipped her onto her side, locked his groin to her round ass and drove into her tight pussy from behind. The new position got him deeper. He also reached between her legs and located her stiff, slick nubbin.

As he circled her clit with his fingertip, she twisted her face. He kissed her briefly and moved his mouth to her pulse point. It hammered beneath his tongue.

"I'm going to…shatter!"

"Come on, honey. Come for me. Come on my cock. Let me hear you scream."

She arched and thrashed against his cock and finger. The energy pumping through her tipped into him. Her pussy flooded his shaft, and that knot inside him snapped. He came with her, his mouth at her ear.

"I'm filling you with my cum. Feel that? It's for you. I'll give you everything I have. Everything I own. All of me." He pumped his hips with each slam of his cock, and she twitched in his arms, his name on her lips over and over until it came out as a final panting whisper.

Until this moment, he didn't realize how suffocating and lonely his life was. Dragging in a deep breath of Pippa's heady scent, he shut his eyes and listened to his pounding heart begin to slow.

She dropped her head to his shoulder, and he banded his arm around her. Still joined, neither moved. After a long minute, her soft question reached through his pleasure haze.

"Who's going to pay for that broken door?"

He smiled. "I would have ripped this place apart to get to you. Never doubt that."

She shivered.

Brushing a soft kiss over her shoulder, he said, "Does your brain ever quit analyzing everything?"

"It did a few minutes ago."

He lazily swirled his tongue over the shell of her ear. "Took ya long enough."

She lifted her head. "To do what?"

"Admit your feelings."

"I had you worried, didn't I?" A teasing note hit her voice.

"Nah. I knew I'd get you eventually."

She stilled. "What happens now?"

Ross knew how to fix problems on the ranch. He could repair a tractor and pull a calf. With WEST Protection, he built his company from thin air, shot the company's reputation sky-high, trained men and learned from the best Navy SEALs.

But when it came to Pippa's question, he was at a loss. She didn't have a damn clue how they'd continue working toward a true relationship when they lived in different states. It might as well be different planets.

When he didn't respond immediately, Pippa pulled away. "That's what I'm afraid of too." She scooted to the edge of the bed, leaving his arms empty and his stomach hollowing out.

He started to reach for her, but his phone vibrated with a call. His jeans, still around his knees, made getting to the phone difficult. "Yeah?" he half-barked at Boone.

"There's a woman in the hotel lobby asking for Pippa's room."

He tipped off the bed to his feet and yanked up his pants in the same move. "What's her name?"

"Meredith."

"Shit. I'll let her know."

Pippa was already pulling her clothes on when he ended the call and faced her. "What was that about?" she asked.

"Your friend's in the lobby."

Her brows shot up into the tousled hair tumbling over her forehead. "What friend? Meredith?"

He nodded.

"Oh my God. She didn't tell me she was coming to Seattle! I bet she showed up to support me because she thinks I've been sick!" She jerked her top over her head and then tore it off again. "I need a shower, but thanks to you, I can't get into the bathroom without severing an artery."

He rounded the bed and took hold of her shoulders. She met his stare. "I can't let you go down there alone."

She rolled her eyes. "Duh."

"You're in danger."

"I remember."

His phone rang a second time. He listened to Boone for a minute and then ended the call. "Boone says your friend went with some others into the bar. We'll meet up with them there — after we shower."

She gaped at him. "You've kept me prisoner in this room for hours, with someone standing guard outside my door. Now I can just waltz into a bar filled with people?"

"I'll be there, along with every man in WEST Protection, Roman and a handful of former military they rounded up in the Seattle area. Taking you into the bar is still risky, but it can also draw out the person behind your attacks."

"Putting innocent people in jeopardy. I'm not sure I want to do this."

"Trust me, honey. We can do this."

She cocked her hip outward, enticing him with the lines of her naked body. "How do you plan on getting into the bathroom to shower?"

He still had on his boots.

"Like this." He swept her into his arms and carried her across the room, stepping over the broken glass and into the bathroom suite.

"I can't believe you didn't even take off your boots for sex."

He grinned down at her, still cradled in his arms. "I'm your bodyguard—I've gotta be prepared at all times."

Her eyes glowed as she curled her hand around his nape and drew him in. "You're my cowboy too."

His heart gave a jog at her words and overflowed with emotions for her. He was in big trouble with this woman.

And his family'd never let him live it down.

* * * * *

Thank God for Ross's sister. If Pippa was going to die today, she'd look great doing it.

She'd never worn deep red in her life. She didn't like sticking out, so she veered toward neutrals for her wardrobe. But she couldn't deny she felt like a model in the sheath dress that hugged her curves and made her legs look even longer. Ross took one look at her and the hunger in his eyes suggested he changed his mind about going to the bar.

When they stepped out of the hotel room, he kept a protective hand on her spine. Boone gave her a long, slow perusal, from her simple black heels to her hair, which she'd brushed until shiny waves fell down her spine.

"Nice to see you, Pippa."

She smiled at him. "You too."

His stare went on. Ross cleared his throat, shifting Boone's attention from her. Whatever he saw on his brother's face made Boone grin, waving a hand toward the short corridor leading to the elevators.

"We've secured the elevator for you. It won't stop at other floors, so nobody else can get in." Boone fell into step behind her and Ross as they started down the corridor.

She felt like the filling of a hot cowboy bodyguard sandwich. Both men rocked jeans and boots like nobody else could. Ross had on a white button-down dress shirt, which she'd watched him iron himself on the setup he found in the hotel closet, and she still felt the effects of watching a gorgeous, half-naked, muscled man ironing his own shirt.

Boone wore chambray with pearl buttons that she'd forever associate with Wynton men. And both of their white Stetsons topped off their appearance.

They stepped into the elevator, and Boone hit the button for the ground floor and bar. She backed up against the wall, bubbles of fear hitting her stomach for the first time since she heard they were going public.

What if someone attacked her? She didn't want bystanders being shot. Meredith. Other friends and colleagues. The Wyntons. Ross.

He caught her gaze and held it. She grew aware of Boone watching them.

"Never thought I'd play the role of elevator man," Boone said to break the strain rising between them all.

She turned to him. "What did you think you'd be when you grew up, Boone?"

"An astronaut."

For some reason, that struck them all as funny, and when they walked out of the elevator, they were all laughing.

Ross sobered first, and his arm vibrated with tension as he guided her a few steps to the bar.

Through the smoky glass windows, she saw people seated around tables, talking and laughing. Others stood in clusters. She couldn't make out any faces until they stepped through the door.

Immediately, she picked out several other white hats and knew Ross's team had a stronghold on the place. She relaxed a fraction, following Ross. Halfway to the bar, she spotted Meredith's blonde hair and broke free of Ross.

He caught her wrist and swung her to him.

"I'm going to talk to my friend."

"Not without me."

"Fine. I'll introduce you." She hurried forward.

Meredith turned and stopped mid-conversation with a man Pippa knew, from other industry events, worked for a pharmaceutical company. Meredith's eyes widened as her gaze fell on Pippa.

At Pippa's back, she felt Ross's familiar body heat vanish. Glancing over her shoulder, she saw him slow his steps. Then in one long stride, he was with her again, leading her up to Meredith.

"Oh my God! Pippa! I hardly recognize you out of your lab coat and ponytail. You look stunning — and healthy! That flu medicine must have really done the trick!" Meredith embraced her.

Being much taller than Meredith always made for an awkward hug, but she wouldn't miss the chance to connect for the world. She squeezed Meredith.

"Thank you for checking in on me. And for the email. It really brightened my day and helped me feel better."

Meredith smiled but got distracted by Ross standing behind Pippa. Who wouldn't? The man's presence was as imposing as a monument.

Twisting to include Ross, she caught his guarded expression...but something more. His brows were pinched and he didn't seem eager to interact with her friend. What did Pippa expect? He was just being overly protective and suspicious.

"Meredith, this is Ross." She was looking at Meredith when she introduced them, so her friend's gaze skittering away from the big man definitely drew Pippa's notice.

Feeling odder by the second, she watched Ross when she said, "This is my friend Meredith."

"Nice to meet you." He spoke with no feeling or warmth at all. He didn't offer a hand to shake.

Meredith drew up her shoulders and thrust them straighter, head held high. "Nice to meet you too."

Was it Pippa's imagination that her friend's voice sounded just as dull and lifeless as Ross's? Maybe they were both being protective of her. Meredith never did tend to like Pippa's boyfriends and didn't hold back about letting her know either.

"Ross is an old family friend. We ran into each other and I invited him to join us for a drink. I hope you don't mind, Meredith."

"Of course not. And look at that—my glass is empty. Follow me to the bar, Pippa, and I'll buy you a glass of wine."

"I'm right behind you." She started after Meredith. Someone touched her arm, and she looked up to see Ryan Letters with another lab assistant.

"Pippa. Wow. You look…" Ryan lifted a hand to scratch at his hair. "Amazing."

She wished everyone wasn't so shocked that she could clean up and look nice. Was she really that much of an ugly duckling?

Also, she couldn't think of anything worse than Ross meeting Ryan Letters. She waved toward Meredith, who'd already reached the bar. "I'm just going to…catch up."

He started to nod, when Ross thrust a hand at him. "Ryan Letters. My name's Wynton."

She expected *and I'm your worst nightmare* to follow, but Ross only glared down at Ryan until he shrank away without ever shaking Ross's hand.

She grabbed Ross's forearm and towed him away, but not before she saw Josiah move in from some corner of the room to keep an eye on Ryan.

"Tell me you didn't come down here to terrorize all my coworkers," she muttered at Ross from the corner of her mouth.

"Of course I did. What did you expect? One of them has it out for you, Pippa."

As they reached the bar, Meredith shot Ross a side-eyed glance. "Your friend can't get his own drink?"

"No, he can't." Ross's voice gritted out with enough force to cause several people on the stools around them to halt their conversations. He jerked his jaw toward the bartender. "Jameson for me and a white wine for the lady."

She arched a brow at him highhandedly ordering her a drink without knowing her preference, but she wasn't about to argue with the stubborn man here. No matter that she actually did prefer white wine to red. Her mother always drank it too, and he might have ordered it because he remembered.

Smiling in thanks at the bartender, she turned to Meredith. "It's sooo good to see you. What a long few days I had out of the lab. Anything new?"

Ross hovered over her and would make anyone nervous. No wonder Meredith wiggled on the barstool. Then she nearly tipped over her own drink. A bit sloshed onto the paper napkin it rested on.

Pippa brought the wine to her lips. From the corner of her eye, she saw Ross knock down his whiskey in one swallow. He stood behind her like the bodyguard he was, but she wasn't a Kardashian and his presence was drawing more attention to her. She knew these people—worked with many of them—and they would be asking why he was glued to her.

"Let's find a table. It will be more comfortable." She slipped from the barstool, drink in hand, and twitched her head for Meredith to follow.

As they moved through the bar, she became aware of Ross motioning to one of his men. When his cousins dropped into seats around a table near the one Pippa chose, she wasn't surprised. Neither wore the statement white cowboy hats, so at least nobody would connect them with Ross. But she still felt more than odd about all this protection.

It also made her edgier about being in the open. After all, she'd suffered an attack in the women's restroom, in a parking lot outside a rest stop and on the highway to Seattle. She didn't relish the thought of another threat to her life.

Ross and Meredith settled across the table from each other. Pippa caught a glower from Ross and directed a kick at his leg under the table. *Stop it,* she tried to convey with her eyes.

And Meredith had somehow finished her drink between the bar and table. She waved for the waitress to bring her another. Her behavior was so...odd.

Pippa was a scientist — making observations came as second nature to her only to breathing, and Ross and Meredith were both tense. While Pippa wasn't a great reader of humans, she did see Meredith jiggling as though she bounced her foot beneath the table. And Ross folded his arms over his broad chest.

Her friend received her fresh drink and instead of sipping it, she gulped. Feeling more off-kilter now,

Pippa attempted to make conversation. She wished Ross would go away for a few minutes and let her speak to her friend alone. It was obvious he made Meredith nervous.

"How was your trip here?" she asked Meredith.

"Fine. Uneventful. You?"

Ross narrowed his eyes on the woman.

Why did Pippa feel she was trapped between two dogs about to go a round over a prized bone? She kicked Ross again. He didn't even move his foot, as though a fly struck his shin rather than the sharp toe of her high heel.

"My trip was good," she said, only half lying.

Meredith turned to her, looking a little frazzled. "How is the wine? I think I'll try some." She waved to the waitress.

Concern burned through Pippa. After a decade of friendship, she'd seen Meredith three sheets to the wind, but it had been a long time. She never drank more than two and was good about cutting herself off. Perhaps she was letting loose because they were out of the lab for the weekend?

"Are you ready for your speech, Pippa?" she asked.

"I think so." She sipped her wine more slowly.

"Everyone is waiting to hear what you have to say. They'll be hanging on your every word." Her words slurred a bit. Pippa threw Ross a glance, only to find he appeared more nervous. He plucked at his shirt buttons and swung his gaze around the room.

More and more out of her comfort zone as the minutes ticked by, Pippa watched her friend down the entire glass of wine. Then she leaned over the table, her cleavage on display. Ross's gaze dropped to her breasts and shot away.

Pippa gaped at her friend — and her lover. Were they attracted to each other? Was that the issue?

When Meredith threw Ross a coy smile, Ross hooked a finger into his shirt collar as if finding it too tight.

Oh my God. They ARE attracted to each other.

"Have you been to Kalamazoo lately, Ross?" Meredith's question made Pippa jerk in her seat and simultaneous choke on her wine. She exploded into a coughing fit while her heart nearly stopped at the realization taking over her brain.

They weren't only attracted to each other — they *knew* each other. Taking in their body clues and the hints dropped by her tipsy friend and Ross evading Pippa's gaze, she could only hypothesize that Meredith and Ross had slept together.

Ross patted her on the back to help ease her choking fit, but she jerked to her feet and took off walking fast across the bar. She had to escape. Why hadn't Ross said anything to her? He'd hidden it from her, and stupid Pippa had fallen straight into his arms after her friend had.

219

A big male body stepped in front of her, barring her way. She tried to skirt around him, but Boone took her by the arm and led her out of the bar. They made it halfway to the elevator before Ross took Boone's place, practically shoving his brother away from her.

"I don't want you right now, Ross." Her icy tone made his green eyes simmer.

"Too. Bad," he said through a clenched jaw.

"Guys? You good?" Boone, caught in the middle, didn't seem to know what to do with himself.

Ross nodded. Pippa shook her head. But then Ross dragged her into the elevator and the doors slammed shut. Enclosed in the small space with the man she'd just declared her love to—who'd also slept with her best friend at some point in Kalamazoo—made Pippa itch to claw the doors open and escape.

Wrapping her arms around her middle, she turned her back on Ross.

"Pippa."

"Save it, Ross. You can't sweet-talk your way out of this."

"What are you talking about?"

She whirled on him as the elevator shot upward to her floor. All she wanted was to lock the hotel room door and crawl under the covers. Pain rocketed around her chest and left her on the verge of tears.

"You lied to me all this time. You slept with Meredith and you didn't tell me." She looked at his face, expecting denial. Hoping for it. But his jaw only tightened, and he said nothing.

Bowing her head, she ignored him all the way to her floor. When he tried to take her by the elbow and lead her to her room, she jerked from his touch. Noah stood at the door as guard. One glare from Ross sent him stepping aside to allow them to pass. Ross produced a room key card and opened the door.

When Pippa stepped through, she tried to shut him out, but he shouldered his way inside and kicked the door shut behind him.

She had to get away from him, and since the bathroom wasn't an option with its door still smashed out, she had the choice of facing him down and learning the cold, hard facts about the man she loved withholding information from her, or head to the balcony.

She rushed across the room and unlocked the balcony door with a rough twist of her fingers. Then she stepped out into the cold Seattle air.

* * * * *

Jesus Christ on a biscuit. What were the odds that he had a one-night stand after meeting a woman in a tech convention in Kalamazoo, and that woman was Pippa's friend?

He'd been off-duty for the night. He thought to have a nightcap after a long day of working security, where several bigwig billionaires required bodyguards. When he took the woman eyeing him up from the end of the bar to his room, he didn't even know her name.

In fact, until the minute Pippa tapped her on the shoulder and he saw her face, he still hadn't known her name. She was nothing to him, then or now. He hardly recalled more than a quick fuck, and then he'd sent her on her way.

"Pippa."

She didn't turn or speak.

"I told you not to come out here."

She stood at the rail of the balcony, back to him. "You slept together." Her voice, already quiet, was softer in the wind.

He stepped up behind her. Aching to pull her into his arms.

"You don't deny it," she said.

"No. But I didn't know her name. It was one night at a convention I was working."

"I don't know why Meredith would attend a tech convention. She works in gene studies with me."

He processed that but said nothing. "Honey...listen to me. Nothing's changed between you and me." He took her by the shoulder and turned her to face him.

The wildness haunting her eyes made him flinch, but he held her stare and bore the brunt of her fury. When she stepped up to him, grabbed him by the neck and yanked his head down to her, shock flared inside him.

Staring into his eyes, she gritted out, "You are not hers."

"Fuck no."

"You are mine." Her anger hit him full force in her kiss. She crushed her mouth to his, and he stepped against her, trapping her to the balcony wall. Her soft body in that red dress had him wanting to rip it off her since the minute she donned it. She tore at his buttons and he practically shredded her dress getting the zipper down.

Their mouths slammed together again and again in an all-consuming claiming. He couldn't get enough. She whipped his shirt off and raked at his shoulders as she stepped out of her dress and climbed up him like a tree on the Wynton Ranch.

His hands shook as he wound her long hair around his fist and tipped her head to get to her throat. He sucked at her pulse point and raked her ear with his teeth. With a cry, she managed to free his cock.

He took himself in hand, the length thick and pulsing. She dropped her panties.

Christ, she was so beautiful. Strong and smart and everything he could ever want in his life. The only woman he could see himself with from this moment on.

Staring into her eyes, he lifted her and thrust his cock into her pussy. She screamed. Not holding back. Her cry was snatched by the wind and carried off into the world as a war cry, as if she fought for Ross and won. But didn't she know he only wanted her?

"I love you," he said at her ear as he jerked his hips. Her walls clenched on his cock, trying to hold him, but it felt too good not to pull out and push inside again.

She gulped in another groan and rocked against him. "I love you too, you damn idiot man."

"I am an idiot. I should have waited my whole life for you."

"Damn right," she rasped, her body going boneless in his hold, telling him she was on the edge of release.

He kissed her again, pummeling her plump lips, forming them to fit his and making her his. His balls swung forward on the churn of his hips. As the tip of his cock buried deeper in her wet heat, he lost his damn mind.

She cried out in bliss. His growl rumbled up from the pit of his soul as the first spurt of cum filled her. He hoped it coated her walls and found its way to her womb. He wanted a family with this woman. To bind them forever.

Her pussy tightened with each contraction of her orgasm. Her lips stole over his as the passion went on and on.

"Ross! Where the fuck—" Boone's voice invaded his sexual haze.

Realizing his brother stood behind him, staring at his bare ass, he twisted free of Pippa's kiss to look at him. Shielding her nakedness from Boone, he said, "What do you need?"

"The guys have that Letters dude locked up in an office and are interrogating him. Thought you might want to be there."

"Gimme a minute," he grated out.

Boone's footsteps faded, and Ross listened for the room door to shut before he withdrew his cock from Pippa and let her slide to her feet. She shivered at the wind hitting her bare skin, and he bent to scoop up his shirt and drape it over her shoulders. She still wore her high heels and nothing else. Her hair disheveled and her eyes alight with a mix of bliss, fury and pain, he couldn't stand to tear himself away from her right now.

But he needed to hear what Letters had to say. His men must have a damn good reason for removing him from the bar and locking him up to interrogate him.

Still, Ross stood there gazing into Pippa's beautiful eyes. "I love you. You know that."

She nodded.

"I have to go."

"I'd like a few minutes alone anyway." She stepped around him through the open French doors.

He grabbed a black T-shirt from his bag and righted his clothes, settling his hat straight before eyeing her again.

"Boone will be just outside if you need him."

She bit into her lower lip and then set it free.

"I'll be back as soon as I can."

Walking away from her felt like ripping a scab off his soul. But he held on to that wild need that drove her to make demands of his body...to claim him as her own.

Chapter Thirteen

Pippa cleaned up and dressed, but she couldn't erase the feel of Ross's hands on her—his lips on her. The passion and raw need that had driven them on the balcony seemed etched into the pores of her skin.

Part of her.

Working in a scientific field all these years had made her out of touch with a lot of her emotions and clouded her view of the world. Meeting Ross again had shifted all that for her. She hardly knew what to think of her actions a bit ago.

Jealousy and anger fueled her. Love had too. It swept her up into a tempest of emotions she didn't know what to do with, so it all channeled into lust.

She sat on the side of the bed, her mind spinning and yet curiously calm. Ross had surrendered to her as much as she had him, and no amount of one-night stands from his past would break that bond. She couldn't even be mad at Meredith, as she hadn't known what Ross was to Pippa at the time.

She still didn't. Pippa hadn't exactly confided in her friend.

Sitting alone with her thoughts led her through several lanes of feelings, from nervousness at presenting her speech tomorrow and what would happen when she did. Someone still wanted her dead and to lay claim to her findings. Men were still guarding her with their lives.

When the phone rang on the nightstand, she jumped. Throwing a glance at the door, she expected Boone to burst in—again—and order her not to answer it. But the door remained closed.

She reached out and nabbed the phone. "Hello?"

"Pippa, it's Meredith."

Mixed emotions tangled in her throat. "Hi." What did she say to her friend?

"I'm embarrassed. I made a fool of myself drinking too much in the bar. We didn't get to talk at all, and then you ran off. I'm not sure what happened."

"I think you do, Meredith."

Silence met her words. After several heartbeats, she spoke, "I do. You have to understand it was a one-time thing and I didn't know he was connected to you in any way, Pippa." Regret rang in her tone.

"He said as much."

"So he's important to you. I knew it by the way he wouldn't move from your side. I'd like to talk to you in person, Pippa. Is there any way you can come to my room?"

She slanted another peek at the door. "I don't know. Maybe." She chewed her lip in thought. "What's your room number?"

"401."

"Okay. If I don't come down, please don't take it to mean I'm angry. It's just late and I have to be fresh for my speech in the morning." Lying was coming more and more naturally to her, and that wasn't a good thing.

"Of course. I hope to see you, Pippa."

After hanging up, she sat there, contemplating their conversation and whether or not she wanted to talk to her friend and learn her side of the encounter with Ross. She wanted to put this all behind her as quick as possible. She loved them both.

She went to the door and opened it. Boone whipped around to face her.

"Everything okay?"

"Yes. I'm hungry. I wondered if you might get me something to eat."

"I can order room service for you."

She shook her head. "I was really craving Chinese. Would you be able to pick it up at the front desk if I order?"

He gave her a crooked smile. "I guess it's the least I can do."

She smiled in return. "Thanks. I'll let you know when it's ready." She started to close the door. "Oh! Any word about what Ross is doing right now?"

"No." His eyes took on a distant expression she read as he didn't want to say.

"Thanks." She closed the door, counted to a hundred and then opened it again. "The delivery person will be in the lobby in fifteen minutes."

He gave her a Wynton nod, a single dip of his head she often thought the family had picked up from their horses.

When fifteen minutes was up, she opened the door, heart pounding. Sure enough, her plan had worked. Boone was nowhere to be seen, having gone to fetch her food, and she knew Ross and his men were tied up with Ryan Letters.

She quickly slipped out of the room and ran for the elevator. Ross would kill her when he found out she left. For that matter, he'd kill Boone for leaving his post. But surely they'd both understand when she told them it was for the sake of saving a long-time friendship?

She rode down the elevator, heart pounding each floor she passed. When she reached Meredith's floor, she began to step into the hallway.

A cloth whipped over her head, wiping out her vision. She opened her mouth to scream, but a hand like a vise clamped over it, cutting off any sound. She struggled, her Aikido training jumping to the fore. But someone—she could only guess two or more people—bound her hands and feet. She bucked in their arms but was carried off with no sense of direction.

She attempted to scream again, heard the tearing noise of duct tape on a roll and anticipated what was coming next. She might have blacked out for a minute, but next thing she knew, the scent of Seattle filtered through the cloth over her head. A car door slammed. Then another.

Tires whirred on pavement as someone drove her away from the hotel. Away from Ross.

If she died at the hands of her kidnappers, it was her own damn fault. But Ross would never forgive himself for it. She couldn't give up—she had to fight her way back to him.

* * * * *

Ross leaned over the table, his glare directed at the douchebag Ryan Letters. The man hadn't told them a thing yet, other than yes, he did have a thing for Pippa. He always did. At that point, he broke down in tears and told them his ex-girlfriend had found him stalking through photos of Pippa in a work setting and called it quits.

Disgusted, Ross straightened. Behind him, someone knocked on the door. He twitched his head toward Noah, who went to see who it was.

"Fuck. What are you doing here? You're supposed to be with Pippa."

Ross swung around at Noah's words, his gaze landing on Boone. His brother's face was ravaged with anguish, and Ross's heart flipped end over end,

231

like that vehicle they'd run off the road on the highway.

In two steps, he grabbed Boone by the shirt front. "What the hell happened?"

"She sent me for food and now she's gone."

"For—" His throat clamped off the rest of the sentence and reopened on his bellow. "She sent you for food and you left? Jesus Christ! Find her!" He stormed from the room, Ryan Letters forgotten as he ran to the elevator. A quick sweep of the floor and her room came up empty.

He grabbed his phone. "Silas, get on the security footage. I want a man at every exit in this place. How the fuck did she slip past us? You all better start looking for jobs, because you're fucking fired!"

Fear pounded through his veins. He could barely draw air. Gone? Where?

Meredith.

He knew her room number after meeting up with her in the bar, and he raced to her door. When he pounded on it and got no response, he kicked it in. Meredith wasn't here either. The room was empty.

His brain pieced the puzzle together. She kept calling Pippa. She acted as a concerned friend, but what if she really was the evil behind the threats and attacks? Pippa said herself it was odd that Meredith attended a tech conference, a fact that wasn't lost on Ross. It could mean she didn't know her friend as well as she thought she did. It also gave Meredith a knowledge of technology that might get her into Pippa's phone and laptop — and them out of this hotel without WEST Protection knowing.

He froze in place, fists clenched at his sides. Terror and shock and fury throbbing through his system. How would he find her? He had to find her.

He stuffed the comms device in his ear and bellowed at his team. "Man every exit. I want footage of the building inside and out. Stop all flights leaving Sea-Tac..." A thought hit him. "And get the authorities to the ports. They might try to get her out of the city by water." He clicked off, sprinting for the stairs. "Goddammit!"

Where to even start? He didn't know which way to turn. As he hit the bottom of the staircase and whirled around the landing to the next, he came up against Boone. Chest heaving, he faced his brother.

"I'm so goddamn sorry, man. I know you love her. This is my fault. Tell me what to do."

Ross's eyes blurred momentarily with tears and then cleared. "I don't know. I can't think where to start."

"We need a lead." Boone took control of the situation. "C'mon." They took the stairs to the ground floor at a deadly pace, hurtling forward.

"I got something. The footage is blacked out, as if someone knew when to cut power to the camera, but it comes on again as a car drives away. The times mesh with the time Pippa went missing." Silas's voice overlapped with Josiah's as they filled in the puzzle for Ross.

"The car?"

"Black sedan."

"Plates?"

"Hard to see in the footage. I'm running it through the program now," Silas told him.

Ross found no hope in what his team told him. He could only think of Pippa getting carried away and how frightened she must be. Sure, she knew how to fight, but anybody could be disabled easily if blindsided.

"License isn't coming up," Silas said.

Ross and Boone exchanged a look. "The fake plates," Ross said.

Boone nodded.

A whoop sounded in Ross's earpiece that could only come from a Wynton. Josiah's voice penetrated his head, each word dropping into him like nuclear warheads.

"I've got eyes on the car. It's traveling west. Ross, I think you're right—they're taking her to a port."

* * * * *

Pippa's lungs burned with the need for air. She didn't relish the thought of going out by suffocation, but she teetered dangerously close.

The hood over her face and the strong tape around her mouth cut off too much oxygen. A dozen biology classes told her that adrenaline would only boost her heartrate, which demanded more oxygen in her veins to keep it beating.

She had to calm down.

All the meditation taught by Tibetan monks and her Aikido training with Japanese masters couldn't stop the panic sweeping through her, though.

Would she ever see Ross again? Her family? She started to think of Meredith—her oldest, dearest friend—but that only took her heartrate higher.

Meredith was behind all of this. The moment someone threw her into the car, she clearly heard Meredith's voice and her order to take her to the dock.

She still couldn't totally believe it. Her friend left her those death threats? Sent someone to attack her in the airport and several other times on the trip to Seattle? She also knew exactly where Pippa was at all times—she'd probably grown savvy enough with technology to infiltrate her laptop with the tracking software. Maybe her phone too.

She had no intention of Pippa reaching Seattle alive.

Pippa poked her tongue between her lips and wiggled it back and forth over the fabric over her mouth. She needed to make a pocket of space where more air could rush in, and she found when she wet the cloth, the tape seemed to loosen. If she could find enough saliva in her dry mouth, she might be able to remove some of the tackiness from the tape.

As she worked at the cloth with her tongue, she took stock of the rest of her body. She sat somewhere hard, probably on concrete or asphalt. Her ankles were bound tight. Her hands tighter. When she attempted to move them at all, a tough plastic dug into her flesh.

Zip-ties.

She wore no coat, and a brisk wind cut through the fibers of her sweatshirt, making her shiver. Which in turn took more oxygen.

She gulped for breath, found little, and panic hit. A scream bottled in her throat. Tears burned on her tongue.

If she cried, her nose would clog off and so would her air. She could...not...cry.

Nearby, someone was smoking. The scent of tobacco carried to her on the wind.

Testing the bindings on her wrists again, she racked her brain to find a way to get out of them. Ropes she could do — she'd done it in her training. But hemp stretched. Even nylon rope had more give than hard plastic zip-ties.

Could the plastic snap with enough force behind it? She had to try. What choice did she have?

She sat there for long minutes trying to gain the courage to fight her way out of this situation. Part of her wanted to give up and just sleep, but she knew that was her need for oxygen. Her mind shutting down.

She drank in a deep breath and slowly inched her knees up, dragging her boots across the gritty ground. She no longer smelled the cigarette smoke and hoped the person had moved away.

When she got her feet into position, she used all her core strength to stand. For a minute, her balance gave way. She tipped. If she fell, she had no way of catching herself and her head would slam off the concrete.

She folded at the waist, fighting for balance and some miracle. Praying for Ross to save her from this situation.

Ross...

She couldn't think of him now. She had work to do.

Straightening, she took in a breath as deep as possible and bent her elbows. The pull against her wrists hurt. But she ignored the pain and tried to work free. Long seconds — minutes, hours? — later, she knew the zip-tie was cutting into her skin.

She still had to get out of it.

Drawing her elbows up and back as far as she could, she pulled the plastic even tighter. Then in one hard jerk, she shoved her elbows out and down at the same time, trying to snap the tie.

Nothing happened.

She tried again. Then a third time. By the sixth, she started losing hope. Her lips trembled, and her face started to feel numb from lack of air.

Focus, Hamlin. You got this.

From some deep well inside her, she drew on a reserve of energy. She yanked her elbows out and down, and her hands broke free.

For a minute, she was stunned that she'd done it. Then survival kicked in, and she raised her hands to scrabble at the hood.

As soon as she ripped it away, her hair falling in her face, she spotted the woman standing not far off.

Her stomach pitched with the bile hitting it. Meredith. She didn't want to believe she recognized her voice, but she was right.

"Impressive escape, my friend," Meredith drawled out.

Her feet were still bound. Dropping to the ground, she grabbed a rock, and using the point to dig into the plastic along with the power from years of martial arts, she set herself free. Meredith didn't move to stop her, but a man rushed in from the side and tried to slam Pippa to the ground.

She grabbed his forearm, hooked her other behind his elbow, and using the man's momentum and body weight, she dislocated his elbow.

He screamed and dropped.

Pippa thrust her shoulders back and faced Meredith, only to find the woman was the source of the smoke.

"You smoke too?" The question came out as a low rasp of surprise. In the recesses of her mind, she realized how stupid it was. But the shocks kept hitting her when it came to knowing her friend.

Meredith lowered the cigarette from her lips and gave a hearty laugh. "You're such an innocent, Pippa. Which is why I'm doing this—you'll never survive the cutthroat industry after you deliver that speech and the world knows of your find. People will come after you."

"*You came after me,*" she said with more strength than she felt. Her voice boomed out across what she now saw was a shipping dock. She was on the coast, and a ship was coming in, the big lights glimmering in a V-shaped path on the choppy water.

Meredith dropped the half-smoked cigarette and stubbed it out with her toe.

"Why are you doing this, Meredith? Are you jealous that I made the discovery? You weren't even working on the same project."

"Grow up, Pippa. Stop being so naïve. You want to help people? The best thing you can do is put your research into the hands of someone who can actually do something with it. Something big." She barked out a laugh. "We all know you'll be content with your named as the scientist who found the big breakthrough to change medicine. But there's a lot of money to be made here."

She sucked in a breath. That spam email and the massive sum of money offered to give up her information loomed in her mind's eye.

"Where did you get the money, Meredith?"

"So naïve, like I said. I don't have the money. I know people who do, though."

"I thought we were friends."

"Friends? No. You've been laboring under the delusion that we're friends, but I've hated you since college."

Pain struck her heart.

"All the guys wanted you. You had the long legs and pretty eyes, while I got the stumpy legs and fat ass."

She started to respond that Meredith was curvy and beautiful, as she always had. But those times were gone, and she snapped her lips shut.

"Your mother gave you diamond earrings for graduation. Mine gave me a smile. The other girls all liked you better too. You were the one getting invited to parties. I just tagged along. Same with the professors. They only saw you, Pippa, while I was always invisible, standing in your shadow."

"None of that is my fault." She raised her head high.

"Of course not. You're just tripping through life in your happy-go-lucky way. You even fell into snagging the best boyfriend, didn't you? Joke's on you, though—I fucked him first. I know how he groans when I put my mouth on his cock."

That bile did rush up her throat this time, and she swallowed hard to force it down. She wouldn't give Meredith the satisfaction of seeing how her words affected her. But deep down, her insides were crumbling into ruin. Their long friendship had been nothing but a scam and a knot of lies.

Meredith lifted a hand and waved at someone. Two more big thuggish men strode forward and grabbed Pippa. She kicked out. She struck one in the throat, and he doubled over, wheezing through a collapsed windpipe. A third man took over for him.

She caught a glimpse of Meredith's retreating back. Over her shoulder, the woman called out in a clear voice, "Bind her again. And make that hood tighter. Then put her in the crate and screw it shut. She gets the slow-boat to China. Bye, Pippa!"

The battle for her life took all her focus, skill and strength. Still, she couldn't escape. She couldn't fight her way to her family. Or to Ross.

They bound her hand and foot, and made damn sure little air and no noises could break through the tape and hood this time. Then they tossed her into a big wooden crate.

The sharp noises of a screw gun trapping her inside was the worst sound she'd ever heard in her life. At least she thought so, until she heard the hydraulics of the crane coming to pick the crate off the dock and load it onto the cargo ship.

She was actually being slow-boated to China. Her only saving grace was the knowledge she wouldn't survive the journey.

Chapter Fourteen

Ross ripped off his hat and slammed his fingers through his hair. Goddammit, what had he done? Allowed the woman he loved to be kidnapped. He'd failed her—after she came to him for protection, he'd failed her.

Not only her. He broke her family. His too. If he didn't get her back, none of them would ever be the same.

He slammed a hand off the dash. "Drive faster, Boone!"

His brother said nothing. Tight-lipped and drawn, Boone must be feeling the effects of his error the way nobody else could. He was the one stationed in front of her door, and she'd appealed to the friend in Boone and asked him to get her food.

"From this day on, we don't take on friends or family," Ross grated out.

Boone said nothing. He only drove, making insane turns through the city at dangerous speeds to reach the coast.

A sick dread surged through Ross. If they hurt her…or worse… Well, he'd never considered himself the serial killer type, but he would hunt down each and every person associated with this act until their DNA was scourged from the Earth.

"We'll get her," Josiah said from the back seat. "We'll get her, Ross."

He didn't reply—he couldn't. His damn throat was constricted, choking off all his air.

As they reached the docks, he spotted the search dogs unit first. WEST Protection had never worked with K-9 handlers before, and he hoped to hell he didn't need to give them direction, because he didn't have the ability to lead right now.

Boone parked haphazardly and cut the engine. Ross hit the ground first, jogging to the group gathered to help them search every inch of the docks to find Pippa.

Approaching the team, Boone pulled out a pair of woolen gloves. With a shock, Ross realized they belonged to Pippa—Corrine had purchased them for her, and somehow Boone had the wherewithal to bring something with her scent to help the dogs find her.

He stared at the gloves, thinking of Pippa's soft fingers. The way she worked them through the strands of her hair as she gathered the mass into a ponytail. And how her hands felt on his body.

He shut down — he had no fucking choice but to bury his emotions and switch to his professional face.

The handlers passed the gloves between them, letting the dogs sniff them and imprint the scent of her on their noses. The chopper Ross had called in flew overhead, sweeping the ground below for signs of that vehicle or Pippa.

"All the ships are docked or floating just offshore, Ross." Boone didn't quite meet his gaze.

"None got out before we closed things down?"

Boone's mouth tightened, drawing brackets around each corner. "One. The Coast Guard's been called out to bring it in."

He gave a stiff nod. "Now we search."

The search crew already dispersed, working the dogs through shipments sitting on the dock to be loaded, and then they searched the ships themselves. Nothing would go unsearched.

Ross jerked his jaw toward Boone. "Let's go."

Josiah and the rest of the team split up to do the same, all of them silent and withdrawn.

Beyond the bright lights illuminating the area, the world looked black. Bleak. Darkness swallowed everything but this circle of the universe, and he hoped to hell Pippa was still in the light.

He thrust away his heavy thoughts and took off with Boone. As they reached a massive flat of heavy metal pipe, he shined his flashlight into one. It was large enough to hide a woman.

245

A body.

No, goddammit. She's alive. I won't fucking believe otherwise.

He and Boone rushed through searching each pipe and found them all empty.

Into his ear, Noah's voice sounded. "Found two guys hiding in a truck. They claim to be homeless and sleep here, but we're taking them in for questioning."

"Let me know what you find out." Ross leaped off the flat holding the pipe and Boone landed beside him. They rushed to the next shipment and the next. When they reached the crates, some of the dogs and handlers were milling around, and the spotlight from the chopper swept the area.

He pointed to a large wooden crate. "Open it," he commanded one of the dock workers who loaded the crates onto ships.

Immediately, two men leaped to action with crowbars and screw guns. As the final screw was removed, Ross stepped up to the crate. He and Boone helped move the heavy wood side.

Holding his breath, almost dying inside, Ross shined his light on the opening.

Bags of cotton fabric filled the entire crate from top to bottom.

"Get a dog here to search."

A handler ran forward with her dog.

It went on and on for what felt like hours but couldn't be more than a few minutes.

"The Coast Guard just radio'd in, Ross." Josiah's voice flooded into his ear. "They located the cargo ship. It left an hour before the port was closed. We don't have long before it reaches international waters."

He and Boone exchanged a look, the first straight-on full stare since they discovered Pippa was missing.

"I'm pinning my money on the cargo ship. Meredith and whoever she's hired would know we'd search the port and they'd get Pippa out as quick as possible. Get me on a chopper, dammit! Now!"

His team went into a flurry of activity and talk. Ross's mind glazed over, his terror for Pippa hitting new heights. If she was on that ship, he could only guess at the traumas she'd received. Beaten, tied up…

"Ross, the chopper's ready!" Boone's bellow in his ear shook him from his dark thoughts, and he jerked around to see the chopper had landed on the dock. Boone gripped his shoulder and looked into his eyes. "I'm sorry, man. So fucking sorry."

"You're not at fault. No one is. But we're both getting her back. You're coming—I need you on my six."

Boone's eyes lost some of the strain, and he gave a nod. They took off for the chopper, and in seconds were in the air, speeding from the dock.

Toward the cargo ship. Toward Pippa.

Christ, he prayed they were on the right track. With his head bowed, he shut out the noise of the

247

chopper and the pilots' talk. He stopped listening to his men on the ground and word that yet another area had been searched and Pippa wasn't found.

His gut told him she was on this cargo ship. He'd never performed an air drop to the deck of a moving ship before, but he was prepared to freefall if it meant reaching her.

Boone nudged his arm. Ross glanced up.

"Christ, Ross. Don't look at me that way."

He didn't ask what way—he knew his heart and soul were somewhere out there, alone and afraid.

"The pilot says the winds are right, and he can fly low enough that we can make a short jump to the ship. The Coast Guard is boarding it as we speak."

"Jesus Christ." He started to stand, and Boone pulled him down.

"We're three minutes out. Are you up for this? You can't make any mistakes, Ross."

"I know it."

"Get out of your fucking head right now."

Boone's harsh command infused his backbone with the steel he needed. When the three minutes were up, and the pilot gave the word, Ross moved to the opening. Wind cut across him and snatched away his hat. Well, that was one casualty lost at sea, and he wouldn't be another.

When he made the jump, his gaze was locked to the deck. His feet struck hard, and he tumbled into a roll. Boone touched down behind him, and Ross leaped up, instantly ready to fight, to kill if need be.

"Start the search," he said to Boone and the men from the Coast Guard standing in front of him. "Time is running out."

* * * * *

Pippa's cheek dug into the rough, splintered wood beneath her. She lay on her side, the thrum of the vessel moving through the water her only link to reality.

Her mind played tricks on her. She thought she heard Ross's voice. It echoed through her skull, took over her pulse. Their last moments together slammed her from all angles, until she could almost feel his arms around her.

I can't give up. I have to reach him.

She shoved herself into a sitting position. Scooting against the wall of the container she'd been locked inside, she battled to find a way out. She slapped her head against the wood. It created a hollow ringing noise.

Could anybody hear that?

She did it again. And again. When her head started to hurt, she used her feet, lifting them and throwing them down on the floor of the crate over and over again.

As kids, she and the Wynton boys had played war in the woods bordering the ranch. She and Ross

249

had escaped capture, and they lay on their bellies, hushed into silence and evading the footsteps of the other kids searching for them.

Ross had begun to tap a finger on the ground, and when she looked at him in question, he whispered, "Morse code. Do you know it?"

She shook her head.

He tapped the ground and said, "A." She imitated him, through the entire alphabet until she knew it forward and backward and inside out.

The rhythm of her boots changed. She tapped out an S-O-S. Again and again. If nobody heard her, then at least she'd tried. She hadn't gone down without a fight for her life.

Inside the hood and tape, she got little air. Dizziness was her constant companion. It made her imagine things. She and Ross riding horses, galloping across the majestic fields of the Wynton Ranch. The wind in her hair.

In her mouth.

A ripping sound hit her ears first, and then the shouts filtered in. The hood left her face, and she didn't think to gulp in until cool air rushed across her lips.

Strong arms lifted her off the floor. She tipped against a hard chest, her head lolling.

"Pippa! Pippa, wake up!"

Ross.

What a sweet dream. She didn't want to wake up.

"Pippa, goddammit, wake up!" The command broke through her haze, and she cracked an eye. Bright lights shot straight to her brain stem, jolting her. She thrashed, and the person holding her crushed her more tightly to his chest.

She gasped in a deep breath and flooded her nose with Ross's scent.

"Get a medic!" he bellowed. "Cut these fucking ties off her!"

His arms never left her as people freed her arms and legs. A plastic mask hovered over her face, delivering precious oxygen her body had been starved of.

Slowly, everything came into focus — first, Ross's face.

Tears overflowed as she centered on his rugged features and knew she was alive — and he was the reason for it.

She hardly registered being transferred to another ship, this time outside of a shipping container. She was not being slow-boated to China. Had they caught Meredith?

Ross sat on the deck, his spine pressed to the side. She lay across his lap, head tucked under his chin. She pulled away. "It was Meredith."

His eyes sparked. "I know."

"Did you catch her?"

251

"There's a manhunt taking place." His gaze moved over her face and fell away. He didn't look at her again.

The tendon in the crease of his jaw flickered, and she knew Ross's rage when faced with it. Pulling out of his hold, she sat up in his lap.

"Ross."

His jaw set more firmly.

"Ross. Look at me."

He didn't.

"I know you must be angry with me for leaving the room. I needed to talk to Meredith — to get closure about what happened between you two."

His gaze jerked to hers and skittered away.

With a shock, she realized he wasn't angry with her — he was stuck in his own head. Battling with himself.

She grabbed his face and forced him to meet her gaze. "Ross, it's okay now. You found me. I'm here. I'm safe now."

His stare penetrated her deep. His chest gave one heave and then he issued a shuddering sigh. He flexed his arms around her, crushing her against him, and she didn't want to be anywhere but here.

His lips moved over her hair. "I'm so sorry, honey."

"You found me."

"Because you were tapping out S-O-S in Morse code."

She blinked. "I thought that was a dream."

He kissed her brow. "No, it was real. You helped me find you. Thank God I found you."

A pair of denim-clad legs moved into her field of vision. She followed the long legs up to Boone's face. "We dock in five minutes."

Ross nodded. Boone started to turn to go.

"Boone," she called out.

He swung back.

"Thank you." Her voice came out as a croak.

He gave her the Wynton nod. The dipping motion put tears of relief in her eyes at the thought of seeing them all again. And her own family too.

Ross drew her head down to his chest. "Don't ever scare me like that again, woman." His grumble vibrated through her.

She found his arm and clamped her fingers on it. "We have a problem now, Ross."

He met her eyes. "What's that?"

"One of us is going to have to quit our job— because we can't be parted. Ever again."

He swooped in, and the soft brush of his lips on hers lifted her heart on wings of love.

Epilogue

Ross let the door of the conference room slam behind him. The noise echoed through the silence of the space, and so did his boots thumping the hardwood floor as he approached the table of men.

Each one had removed his white hat, and they set on the table before them. Several raised their heads as he neared. Some, like Boone and Josiah, had their heads bowed in contemplative silence.

He pulled his hat off—his second best since his first was lost somewhere in those dark waters off the cost of Washington—and dropped it to the surface before he sank to the big leather chair.

One glance at his team, and he knew their morale was busted. They had some wins and losses during this mission to save Pippa. It wasn't his job to tell them off for the things they did wrong. Right now, he had to lift them up, fortify them to go out and do it all over again tomorrow.

"Let's talk about our new hires. Noah?" He received several surprised glances at opening with a topic they didn't expect.

His little brother met his stare. "I've made one new hire working under Silas in cybersecurity."

Ross lifted his pen. "Great news. We need another good man. What's his name?"

"Lauralee Sheldon."

Their heads all snapped up. Ross bobbed his head. "Good. We need diversity on the team too. I look forward to meeting our new hire. Tell her she starts in the morning."

Noah grinned and gave a nod.

"I also want to share that they've caught the woman responsible for Pippa's attacks and kidnapping—Meredith. She was arrested in a roadblock search leaving Washington state."

"What a relief," Josiah said.

"Now about the Grammys." He let the statement hang in the air for a long moment. "I don't think we're ready to take on the contract, even if it's offered to us."

Nobody spoke.

"If it's because of my screw-up with Pippa, then blame it on me. Don't drag the rest of the team down for my stupid mistake." Boone picked up his hat from the table and dropped it over and over again.

Ross eyed his brother. He'd been withdrawn since the minute they learned Pippa had been taken.

"Ya know, brother," he drawled, "a man once told me to get the fuck out of my head right now, and it was damn good advice. So I'll say it to you now—

get the fuck out of your head, Boone. We all make mistakes. WEST Protection's still new. We might not be crawling like infants but we're barely on our feet, and we have a long way to go. We need your head in the game one thousand fucking percent. Are you with us, brother?"

Boone raised his head and met Ross's direct gaze. He watched the change come over his brother with his speech. "Yeah, I'm with you. *Two thousand fucking percent.* So let's shoot for the Grammys."

"We'll shoot for it then. And if it's a miss, then we try again next year. And the year after that. Until our team is big enough to handle anything. What we did this week was dig deep and discover a greatness among us. What we couldn't handle, we found backup for. Where we faltered, we found someone to pick us up." He settled his attention on Boone again. "Like you picked me up, man. I couldn't have gotten Pippa back without you." He swept his stare over the table. "All of you."

They exchanged smiles and nods, the team bond made tighter by what they'd achieved and stronger because of their shortcomings.

"That brings up a big rule that got broken on this mission. We had a deal when we founded this company that we couldn't sleep with our wards." Landon Trace eyed him.

Silas, the third founder, gave a stiff nod. "Whattaya think, Trace? Do we put him on probation?"

256

Ross held up his hands. "About that. Pippa and I would have hooked up if she'd come to visit. We've been friends since childhood."

"Doesn't change the fact you broke the rules." Landon shot him a grin.

Seeing they were razzing him for stomping all over a set of rules he helped create, he ducked his head to hide a grin. "I'm very sorry for it too."

Silas chuckled. "Damn liar."

Ross looked up. "You're right—I'm not one bit sorry. With that out of the way, let's talk about my feelings."

They all blinked at him.

"What is this? A therapy session?" Boone threw out, to several chuckles.

"I'm in love with Pippa. And she isn't leaving my side from this day forward. While we're all a little rusty with our barn-raising skills, I need all hands on deck, armed with hammers."

"What are we building?" Boone asked.

"A lab," Pippa announced from the doorway.

Ross met her stare and smiled. She returned it and moved into the room, passing each man and stopping to squeeze his shoulder or say a kind word of thanks until she had spoken to each man in WEST Protection. When she reached Ross's side, she rested her hand on his shoulder.

"A lab?" Josiah asked.

"Yes. I don't need a big city to do my research. And now I have enough experience—credentials too—to head my own lab," she said.

"We'll need deep background checks on every person she wants to hire," Ross put in.

She squeezed his shoulder. "Of course. I hope ya'll will welcome a city girl around here."

Boone grinned at her. "You've always been one of us, Pippa. Welcome to the family."

Ross's heart squeezed with affection for his brotherhood seated around him. And for the woman his heart beat for.

"We start on the lab as soon as I get the lumber here. Until then, get to work, guys."

They all stood, except Ross. As soon as they were alone, he drew Pippa around to his lap. She curled into his arms, her soft weight already driving him to the brink.

He nuzzled her throat. "I have to have you. I'm crazy for you, Pip."

She palmed his cheek, rasping her fingertips over his beard stubble. "We've had sex in a lot of odd places. What do you think about a conference table?"

He growled against her throat. In a swift move, he whipped her up to sit on the table and parted her legs, his face on a level with her pussy.

Grinning, she tipped onto one hip and pulled his smashed, second-best Stetson out from under her butt. He groaned as he saw the flattened felt.

"I'm out another hat," he said.

She tossed it across the room. "I'll buy you another, cowboy. Right now, I want your full attention on me." She started working the buttons on her shirt, baring bits of freckled skin to tease him into a bigger state of arousal. As if he needed it— everything she did made him want more and more of her.

Suddenly, he shoved to his feet. His chair hit the wall behind him with a crash. As he gripped her thighs and dragged her to the table's edge so he could grind his erection against her pussy, they shared a moan.

"I love you with everything in me, Ross Wynton." She searched his eyes, her own two like candles glowing up at him.

His chest tightened with a burn it always did when she said the words. "I'll never tire of hearing that."

She whipped open her blouse, exposing her bare breasts. "Will you tire of sucking these?"

"Hell no." He went straight for one nipple, drawing it to a tight bud and then moving to the next. He spread her out on the table and stripped her slowly, savoring every bit of skin as he went.

She dug her fingers into his shoulders, bringing him close until their lips were a breath apart. "I'm gonna like being on the ranch, Ross."

"Mmm. I'll never let you go. Now shut down your brain, woman, and just feel..." He captured her mouth in a long, dizzying kiss that felt like the start of their lives together.

THE END

Don't miss out on Boone's story GUARDED BY THE COWBOY! 1-click yours now at Amazon.

Fake marriage? If that's what it takes to get the job done.

Boone Wynton is one of the top bodyguards on the

WEST Protection team and in the country. So taking a job to protect the wife of a billionaire oil tycoon seems like a breeze—until he learns he can't get near the possessive man's wife unless he's married. His only option? A coworker who hates him. Maybe she is kind of pretty, and her lips drive him crazy—as long as she isn't speaking.

Cybersecurity guru Lauralee Sheldon has worked at WEST Protection all of a month—exactly long enough to learn she can't stand Boone Wynton. The only way she'll act as his fake wife is for the sake of protecting a vulnerable woman, and even then on one condition—that Boone never lays a hand on her, though they are big and perfectly rough.

When fighting turns into foreplay, Boone changes the rules of the game, blurring the lines between real emotions and deception. And with danger flying at them from all directions, it's hard to know who to trust. Is it the man Lauralee never believed in?

BUY YOUR COPY ON AMAZON

* * *

**Interested in Roman and his role with The Guard? Find more at empetrova.com or Amazon.

261

Em Petrova

Em Petrova was raised by hippies in the wilds of Pennsylvania but told her parents at the age of four she wanted to be a gypsy when she grew up. She has a soft spot for babies, puppies and 90s Grunge music and believes in Bigfoot and aliens. She started writing at the age of twelve and prides herself on making her characters larger than life and her sex scenes hotter than hot.

She burst into the world of publishing in 2010 after having five beautiful bambinos and figuring they were old enough to get their own snacks while she pounds away at the keys. In her not-so-spare time, she is fur-mommy to a Labradoodle named Daisy Hasselhoff.

Find More Books by Em Petrova at empetrova.com

Other Titles by Em Petrova

West Protection
RESCUED BY THE COWBOY
GUARDED BY THE COWBOY
COWBOY CONSPIRACY THEORY
COWBOY IN THE CORSSHAIRS
PROTECTED BY THE COWBOY

Alaska Search and Rescue
NORTH OF LOVE
EAST OF FERVOR
WEST OF DESIRE
SOUTH OF HUNGER

Xtreme Ops
HITTING XTREMES
TO THE XTREME
XTREME BEHAVIOR
XTREME AFFAIRS
XTREME MEASURES

Crossroads

BAD IN BOOTS
CONFIDENT IN CHAPS
COCKY IN A COWBOY HAT
SAVAGE IN A STETSON
SHOW-OFF IN SPURS

Dark Falcons MC
DIXON
TANK
PATRIOT
DIESEL
BLADE

The Guard
HIS TO SHELTER
HIS TO DEFEND
HIS TO PROTECT

Moon Ranch
TOUGH AND TAMED
SCREWED AND SATISFIED
CHISELED AND CLAIMED

Ranger Ops
AT CLOSE RANGE
WITHIN RANGE

BODY LANGUAGE
REINING MEN
ROPIN' HEARTS
ROPE BURN
COWBOY NOT INCLUDED
COWBOY BY CANDLELIGHT
THE BOOT KNOCKER'S BABY
ROPIN' A ROMEO

Ménage à Trouble Series
WRANGLED UP
UP FOR GRABS
HOOKING UP
ALL WOUND UP
DOUBLED UP novella duet
UP CLOSE
WARMED UP

Another Shot at Love Series
GRIFFIN
BRANT
AXEL

Rope 'n Ride Series
BUCK
RYDER

RIDGE
WEST
LANE
WYNONNA

The Dalton Boys
COWBOY CRAZY Hank's story
COWBOY BARGAIN Cash's story
COWBOY CRUSHIN' Witt's story
COWBOY SECRET Beck's story
COWBOY RUSH Kade's Story
COWBOY MISTLETOE a Christmas novella
COWBOY FLIRTATION Ford's story
COWBOY TEMPTATION Easton's story
COWBOY SURPRISE Justus's story
COWGIRL DREAMER Gracie's story
COWGIRL MIRACLE Jessamine's story
COWGIRL HEART Kezziah's story

Single Titles and Boxes
THE BOOT KNOCKERS RANCH BOX SET
THE DALTON BOYS BOX SET
SINFUL HEARTS
JINGLE BOOTS
A COWBOY FOR CHRISTMAS
FULL RIDE

Club Ties Series
LOVE TIES
HEART TIES
MARKED AS HIS
SOUL TIES
ACE'S WILD

Firehouse 5 Series
ONE FIERY NIGHT
CONTROLLED BURN
SMOLDERING HEARTS

Hardworking Heroes Novellas
STRANDED AND STRADDLED
DALLAS NIGHTS
SLICK RIDER
SPURRED ON

EM PETROVA
WWW.EMPETROVA.COM